The Fat of the Land

R. Allen Chappell

Acknowledgments

Few books are written alone – my sincere gratitude to all those who contributed information, critiques, and most importantly support.

A special thanks to the Steamboat Writers Group and their guiding light, Harriet Freiberger, without whose help and encouragement this would still be trapped in my head.

Table of contents

Prologue

This collection from the Southwest features the people who give life to that land, the outliers, the poor, and disenfranchised. Some of them you will like ...others you may not.

These narratives are written with a large dollop of literary license. The characters and their names are fictitious and any resemblance to actual persons, living or dead, is purely coincidental. These are their stories, told in the vernacular of the time and culture. No disrespect or offense is intended in the telling.

The Fat of the Land

I was nearly nine years old before I realized we were poor - it came as quite a shock – no one had to tell me, I just woke one morning, and there it was. We were poor. We were caught under the grinding-wheel of poverty and couldn't seem to tear loose. Eventually it wears you down until your hopes, and youth, and whatever dreams you might have, are ground to a fine red dust. The wind picks that up and carries it away, and in the end there is just the sun and the wind and the weight of the wheel.

Route 66 ran right through our town and half the people in the United States passed by at one time or another. They didn't stay long. It was one of those dusty little New Mexico towns at the edge of the *llano*. The sort of town you could spend a lot of time in ...in just a few minutes. Eventually, even the townspeople began drifting away, until there weren't enough left to have a good parade. The Mexicans of course didn't leave. They had been in that country several hundred years and knew no better. *"No le hacén nada,"* they would say, summing things up. They knew it would be pretty much the same for them anywhere else. Good thing too, those Mexicans, turns out, they were all that was left between us, and the bottom rung of the social ladder. I was in the fourth grade, and couldn't read. The Mexican kids couldn't read either. Our old teacher divided us into two reading groups, the Mexicans and me on one side and everyone else on the other. We were issued copies of a book called, "Fun with Dick and Jane," featuring happy storybook children who had pets named Spot and Puff.

They spent idyllic days at play in a mythical neighborhood back East somewhere, with green grass, trees, and soft summer rain. A big adventure, for them, would be for their red wagon to go rolling downhill by itself with Spot and Puff aboard. "Oh dear," Jane would say. They never used strong language even in the worst emergency.

I had a black Chow dog named "Chinky" who would take down a Puff in a heartbeat, and if my wagon should happen to run off downhill by itself, you would have been appalled at the language. Nothing Dick and Jane did or said seemed to relate to the world as I knew it. And, as you can well imagine, the Mexicans were at a total loss. We approached the book from every angle ...*Qué pasó?* But in the end, came to regard it as a mystery. *Espiritos santos!*

In the first part of the fourth grade they had to replace our old teacher, I don't remember why, maybe she moved or got sick, or ...maybe she just wore out and had to be replaced. I can't recall her name now or what she looked like, though I have tried. Teachers looked pretty much the same in those days, at least until Miss Hale came along. Even after all these years I can still see her standing in front of the class for the first time. She looked like a grown-up Shirley Temple – cast in the wrong movie. She was a little nervous, though she covered it well. "Hello class," she smiled, "My name is Miss Hale. I'll be your new teacher. We're going to have a lot of fun in the fourth grade!" Those were her exact words, too. I'll never forget them. Having fun in the fourth grade was the farthest thing from our minds, but the way she said it, made it seem like a viable option. Suddenly, anything seemed possible. Every child in the fourth grade fell instantly in love …and we were forever the better for it. *Gracias a Dios*

She immediately abolished the two-party reading system and shuffled the class around like peas in a shell-game. When the dust settled I was right up there at the front of the class, Kiko Chavez and me – sharing a desk like two different peas in a pod. Kiko had a natural aversion to Anglos that went clear back to the Conquistadors. He had failed a grade somewhere along the line and was somewhat bitter about it; he was also somewhat the bigger for it. He and his gang-of-three had been chasing me home from school for months. Thanks to Kiko, I was the fastest runner at Lincoln Elementary. I don't know how Dick and Jane would have handled it, but I can tell you right now, Spot and Puff would have been the least of their worries.

You would have thought that after a while, Kiko would have given up on catching me; he never came close. One time when I was only a hundred yards or so from home, and well out in front, I pretended to sprain my ankle and began limping noticeably. There immediately came "Ki-Yies" and screams of triumph from behind – Apaches on a blood trail – at the last moment however, I put on a burst of speed, jumping half-grown mesquite bushes and clearing the picket fence in front of our house. I ran inside and locked the screen-door ...casually leaning up against the doorjamb as they screeched up to the front gate. Kiko reached down and picked up a rock, hefting it a couple of times, like he was going to throw it through the screen. But, he knew better.

"We almos' had him this time, Kiko!" I could hear one say.

"Yeah," Kiko lifted one of his shoes and examined the sole. "Look at these tennies man! There's no treads left at all, it's no damn wonder I can' get no traction." He scowled darkly at the house and yelled, "We're gonna' get you next time 'essé' and don' you forget it!" After a few choice expletives they ambled off down the road to their houses across the tracks.

You had to hand it to Kiko; he never gave up. Maybe it was because it was right on the way home anyhow, or maybe he just couldn't help it – like a dog that chases cars. It looked like it might go on for years. I hoped not; I had nightmares of myself, in a business suit, running home from work every night with Kiko right behind me.

My Grandpa said they were just bullies. He told me, next time, I should turn around and hit the biggest one right in the nose; they wouldn't bother me again, he said. It was an interesting theory and I would have loved to see someone try it. But, it wasn't going to be me. I had seen my Grandpa be wrong on a number of occasions.

One afternoon, after a particularly close contest, I was out in the front yard catching my breath and watching Kiko and the boys head out across the tracks. The screen door slammed at the house across the road and I looked up to see Leon Hardey coming over. Leon was sixteen and had quit school the year before. He and his brother Alvin worked on ranches around the country and were considered tough hombres. As usual, he wasn't wearing a shirt, just faded Levis and old run-over cowboy boots. A toothpick dangled from one corner of his mouth and there was a homemade tattoo of a coiled rattlesnake on one bicep, the kind they do in the reform school up at Springer. He slouched up to the gate, put one hand on the side-post, and just sort of floated over the fence, as though that was easier than opening the gate. He didn't say anything, just waltzed over and plopped down in the shade, in one of those old green metal lawn chairs. He yawned and indicated the other chair with his toothpick. I hurried over to sit, though I had some serious reservations – Leon Hardey wasn't much on social calls.

It was said that Leon had "whipped" a full-grown man only the week before. The man, about half-drunk at the time, had been coming out of the Hitching Post Lounge, and accidentally bumped Leon, who had been peering through the doorway at a pool game in progress. Leon stood there waiting for the man to apologize and when he didn't, Leon hit him four times so fast the man didn't have time to fall down. He was a large man and just stood there, out on his feet, until Leon eased him to the sidewalk. They said the man didn't wake up for some time. Leon wasn't mean-natured, but he was a stickler for protocol.

"Old Kiko's lean'n on you a little heavy, ain't he?" He said, looking off down the road toward Mexican town. He had piercing grey eyes and never looked directly at anyone. He pulled out a can of Copenhagen, tapped the lid a couple of times and put a little pinch in his lower lip. We just sat there in the shade for a few minutes while Leon worked up some juice in his chew. A half-grown horny-toad started across the yard on its evening hunt. Leon let it get out a ways, pursed his lips slightly, and let fly a stream that hit it right in the back of the head. I wasn't expecting that, and neither was the horny toad.... It got our attention.

"The thing is..." Leon said, shifting his chew around, "...is that Alvin feels it's a little embarrassing, right here in the neighborhood and all. He thinks them boys might be gettn' a little out of hand. He said maybe I should come over and see could I help you out, seein' how you don't have a big brother."

I didn't know why Alvin should be embarrassed. It sure didn't bother me none. I was born knowing I couldn't whip three Mexicans. I didn't have anything to be embarrassed about.

"Alvin says it's just something we shouldn't let get out of hand." I could see it wasn't open for discussion so just stayed shut-up and waited for further instructions. "Now what I want you to do is ...first thing in the morning, when you get to school, is to tell old Kiko that if I catch them chasing you one more time, I personally am going to beat the crap out of all three of them."

"OK." I said. The plan appeared flawless to me and unlike my Grandpa's, this one involved very little personal risk. Only a fool would defy the Hardey boys and Kiko was no fool.

The next morning, when Miss Hale went back to the supply room, I leaned over to Kiko and whispered, "Leon Hardey says if you chase me home one more time, he's gonna beat the crap out of all three of you!" I could sense Kiko flinch mentally, though he gave no outward sign.

"I ain' scared of Leon Hardey!" he said – but he said it real soft and I knew my running days were over.

When school let out that afternoon, I leisurely put my supplies away, exchanging pleasantries with Winona Hunt, and watching Kiko out of the corner of my eye. No need to be the first one out the door now; I was under the divine protection of the all-powerful Hardey brothers. Wandering out onto the school ground, I spent a few minutes watching the playoffs of the day's marble tournament, the one held over from recess. There were a lot of "high rollers" around and fortunes were being made and lost in a single day. I was startled to see my big red "aggie" in the middle of the circle. Only the week before, I had traded it off in a fit of greed. That aggie had changed hands several times since then and I had lost track of it. All professional marble players had an aggie for their "shooter" ...really... nothing else would do. An aggie was as hard as a rock, which it was, and they were worth a great deal – I don't remember how much, but it was a lot. Some down-on-his-luck tinhorn must have thrown my aggie in the pot in a last desperate effort to recoup his fortune.

Finus Boagard was next up and he was making a big show of running some red dirt through his fingers and tossing his shooter back and forth. Finus was fat and red-faced and wore a big black cowboy hat. His daddy was a cowboy and Finus didn't let anyone forget it. His nose was running, as usual, and he blew it with two fingers, leaving a streak of red mud. Then of course he had to sift some more dirt. Snot and big-time marbles don't mix.

Any time I won marbles from Finus I always washed them in the irrigation ditch.

Kiko had been edging over toward the game and now stood across the circle watching. I had of necessity become a serious student of Mexican psychology. I knew someone was in trouble – I hoped it would be Finus.

Finally, the grandstanding over, Finus got into position to shoot, putting his grubby knuckle slightly across the line.

"Dammit Finus! You're fudging!" an older boy yelled.

"Durned cheater!" a little red-headed girl whispered, shaking her curls.

Finus puffed up his cheeks like a toad and glared around the circle, but he moved his shooter back. Then, expelling his breath in a big whoosh, he fired his marble across to the target, knocking my red aggie clean out of the ring. It was a great shot and no one was more surprised than Finus. It ranked right up there with Leon spitting on that horny toad. As the red aggie rolled to a stop, Kiko reached down and picked it up, bouncing it on his palm as he looked at Finus.

"Hey! That's mine!" Finus squealed, starting to get up.

"Well, come get it then *pendeho*!" Kiko taunted.

Finus sank back down to his knees. "Dadburn it", he said, wiping his face with his hand – arranging the dirt, snot, and sweat, into an interesting collage. He was licked and he knew it. Finus wasn't one to tempt a fickle providence. No one felt sorry for Finus, it was fate, it could happen to any of us, still, we were glad it happened to him.

Kiko seemed disappointed, and turned for home in disgust – taking my red aggie with him. I hated to see Kiko get that aggie but it was better off with him than with Finus. That marble had enjoyed a more exciting life than most kids I knew and I often wonder what finally became of it. Red aggies don't get lost very often and kids don't play marbles anymore – so it's probably hidden away in some old grandpa's sock drawer somewhere.

...I wish I had it.

On the way home I caught up with Kike, but stayed on the other side of the road. A blue haze was settling in along the bottoms where the shadows fell. We didn't say anything, just trudged along separately ...kicking up little puffs of red dust, the day dying softly at our backs. He pulled out my aggie and started tossing it up in the air. He knew it was my old shooter alright. He didn't offer it back of course, and I didn't expect it. I was the one who finally broke the silence. "I didn't tell Leon on you boys!" I didn't want it to get around I was a rat. He just shrugged, concentrating on catching the marble, his face a thousand-year-old Incan mask. It seemed odd for Kiko to be alone.

In the distance I could see Leon sitting on his front porch. He didn't look at us, he didn't have to ...it was just as he knew it would be. Kiko didn't look up as we went by, and neither did I. I felt sorry for Kiko in a detached, lonesome kind of way. It was over now, and he knew this was the way it would always be. *Qué lástima.*

The next morning Miss Hale asked Kiko and me if we would stay in at noon and have our lunch with her. She said we could make a little party of it. (We all brought our lunches in brown bags, and you could buy little cartons of milk – white or chocolate – for a nickel.)

My lunch was never a very elaborate affair, no potato chips, or pickles, or cookies. Mainly, it was just a baloney sandwich on 'Wonder' bread. I made it myself and wrapped it in waxed paper. We didn't have any of those little sandwich size paper bags – we just had the regular big grocery sacks rolled up to fit. All the way to school that baloney sandwich would rattle around in there like a bad dream.

When noontime came, we pulled our desk up to Miss Hale's and unwrapped our lunches. I felt a little embarrassed at first but then saw that Kiko just had a bean burrito. Miss Hale had an egg salad on toasted whole wheat. It was the first egg salad sandwich I had seen. She brought out three cartons of milk and suggested that we each cut our food into thirds and share. "Try some of this egg salad," she insisted.

I started right in on my share. Miss Hale said she hoped she had not put too much paprika in it for us. "No ma'am," I said "I like my egg salad with lots of paprika." Kiko looked at his egg salad a long time. I could tell he didn't know what paprika was either.

"My, this baloney sandwich certainly hits the spot," she said, "and the bread is nice and fresh too."

"Yes ma'am, that's 'Wonder Bread.' I like it a lot better than 'Sunbeam,' it seems to have a better texture... don't you think?" (my aunt Edna always said that, so I just threw it in to make conversation)

Miss Hale nodded thoughtfully. "Its lovely bread."

We all started on our burrito at about the same time. I saw that Kiko had put plenty of green chiles in the refries. Miss Hale's eyes were watering by the time she finished.

Kiko spoke for the first time, "I hope I din' got too much chile on those beans, Miss Hale."

"Oh my goodness no," she replied in a high voice. "I like a lot of chile on my burrito." She finished off the lunch with her egg salad and a carton of milk and was able to talk in her normal voice again. Miss Hale was a natural-born genius with kids – she soon had Kiko and me going on like a couple of magpies, and after a few more pleasantries, got right down to business. "I have something for you boys that I think you are really going to enjoy." She said this as though she were about to bestow a great treasure upon us. Kiko and I looked cautiously at one another. She reached into her desk drawer and brought forth three slim volumes… books!

"I thought it was gonna' be some 'Twinkies' or somethin," Kiko mumbled, obviously disappointed.

It occurred to me that Miss Hale might have us mixed up with a couple of kids who could read. "We can't read!" I said quickly, hoping to clear up any confusion before something bad happened.

Kiko nodded affirmatively. "We couldn' even read, Dick and Jane!" ...laying to rest any shred of doubt.

"Well," she laughed. I think you can read this book, it's, Huckleberry Finn." Kiko looked sideways at me and asked from the corner of his mouth, "Wha's a Hugglebury Finn?"

Miss Hale explained Huckleberry Finn …a boy about our age who ran away from home on a raft and had great adventures, living, as she put it, "off the fat of the land." What she had in mind was a private club, she said, one that would meet every day for lunch and take turns reading about this boy on the river.

Rafts! Running away from home! A private club? I'll say it again: Miss Hale was a genius. She began reading that very day and we were hooked like carp on a dough-ball. It took us quite a while to finish that book... a month maybe. It was harder for Kiko since he did most of his thinking in Spanish and had to sort of juggle the two languages back and forth in his head. When his turn came to read, the sweat would pop out on his forehead. He would grip the book by both edges and a near physical struggle would ensue between him and the English language. Maybe he did it for Miss Hale, or maybe to show me up ...or maybe he just hated to give up.

Kiko had a remarkable memory, and as we walked home in the evening, he would often quote whole passages of the day's reading. It was interesting to hear Huckleberry Finn done in a Mexican accent. It sounded alright somehow.

By the end of the school year we could read as well as anyone else in class. I wish I could say we went on to become great scholars because of it; but that would be a lie. I did however, go on to get a library card and became an obsessive reader, so much so in fact, Miss Hale had to admonish me on several occasions for reading library books during class. She acted real stern about it, but then would turn away to hide a strange little smile. I wish I had kept in touch with her over the years. She really wouldn't be that old... as I reckon age now. I sometimes wonder where she is, or what she went on to do, and how many lives she turned around before she was through.

My reading ability was directly responsible for my first high-school job, radio announcer at our small hometown station. I was on the air that morning, several years later, when the UPI news wire sent across this local item directed just to our region: Dateline—Viet Nam—Private 1st Class, Romaldo "Kiko" Chavez, was killed this week in heavy fighting along the DMZ. His commanding officer stated that Chavez was the last to leave his post, allowing several companions to fall back to safety.

I read the report on the local noon news. Usually there would be calls when we aired such a story; but not this time. The Viet Nam war was winding down and people were sick to death …of death.

Kiko and I never became what you would call close friends, but I always felt someone should have called in. I called the wire service back and had them transfer the story up north to Raton, New Mexico, where Kiko's grandparents lived. Maybe someone called in up there.

Fat of the Land

Ya-Ta-Hei ...Over!

The last time I saw Freddy T'sosi, he was sitting on a bar stool in Aztec, New Mexico trying to drink himself invisible.

He had just returned that morning from a three-day tribal ceremonial down at Window Rock, where he had been morally and financially outraged. His last five dollars was on the bar, and he was still somewhat short of his goal. I could tell he was genuinely glad to see me. Freddy and I went back a long way – high school. He was from over around the Blanco Canyon area, and came to board at the government dormitories during the school year. In those days I had an old red Model A Ford, with the top chopped off, that was nearly twice as old as we were. It looked just like the one in the "Archie" comic books and Freddy seemed to identify it with the all-American teenage dream. He would walk over to the school parking lot at lunchtime and we would sit in the Ford and talk. We became friends after a fashion; though, not much of that was done in those days. I liked hearing about life on the reservation and would press Freddy at every opportunity.

He told me, back in the old days, the government would send the agents out in flatbed trucks, with stock racks, to round up all the school-age kids. The Diné (that's what they call themselves by the way, The People) would try to hide the children or send them back into the canyons to be with relatives. But the agents became very clever after a few years, and would root them out – taking any child, boy or girl that appeared to be six years old, (mothers were not to be trusted in this). They went with only the clothes on their backs; some crying, others stoic, all round-eyed with fear. Many times the agents could not understand their names, so would make up names for them. Thus there came to be Jessie Shorthair, Charlie Redhouse, Bobby Greyhills and others named for physical characteristics or features near where they were picked up. At the school they would be shorn and de-loused like so many sheep. Some of them spoke no English at all. It was hard.

The government has always considered the Navajos an enigma. They do not traditionally live in groups like other tribes. Their land is a barren place where even the coyote has a hard time making a living and it takes many square miles for a single family to survive. Dealing with the Navajos was like dealing with a hand-full of sand. The government would shake its head, clucking like an old hen. "You Navajo," the government would say, "Why can't you stay close by – like good little chicks," but the Navajos appeared not to understand. They continued wandering about wherever their sheep and goats took them. They thought they should do as they had always done. Being a quiet people, who caused no harm, they thought things would work out for the best that way.

The government tried to keep its sense of equanimity, often going out of its way in the matter. Finally though, at wits end, it said, "Enough is enough! We can't have you Navajo going about as you please; what will people think? What you Navajo need, is a good Schooling!" (the government had a plan) "The sooner you Navajos learn to be like everyone else, the better!"

Freddy saw the first couple of years as the toughest. Several times, he tried to run away, but would be caught, digging under the fence, in the same place each time. They would drag him back kicking and yelling. I suppose you could say he became an anarchist in a small way. He would lie awake at night under a blanket that said U.S. Navy – thinking up ways to overthrow the government. He missed his mother and little sister. He also missed his morning coffee: one-third cup strong black coffee – one-third cup sugar – one-third cup 'Pet' canned milk ...regular Navajo coffee. It was a real eye-opener, and when taken with a piece of mutton and hot fry bread, would see you through a full day herding sheep. Oatmeal, toast, and orange juice paled in comparison.

He told me that about the time he got used to three fancy meals a day, clean sheets, and a regular bath, it would be springtime ...time to go back to the reservation. Back to a dirt-floored hogan, greasy fried mutton, canned tomatoes, and lice in your hair.

Out on the reservation it got pretty lonely during the summer. There were no other children his age nearby so most of his time was spent following the sheep and goats around. The coyotes, liked nothing better than finding a herd of sheep and goats with no herder.

Nothing seems to make the time fly for a coyote like a lonely herd of sheep and goats.

Freddy's father had been taken prisoner by alcohol many years before and no one knew where he was being held captive. He had wanted to be a rodeo star, you know, be somebody. Freddy could hardly remember what he looked like, and there were no pictures.

It seemed that Freddy became more and more a stranger each summer. His little sister would follow him around with big eyes. She couldn't seem to keep track of who he was from one homecoming to the next. His mother knew what was happening. She had been to Indian school herself, though it had been a long time back, and she had not taken it seriously. She called him by his Navajo name and talked quietly of how well things were going – how good the sheep had done that winter. She told him, that when he was through school, there might be money for a pick-up truck. She told him he would look good in a Chevy.

After a few years, Freddy no longer seemed to miss his family. It was as though they were someone else's family. He told me he would just as soon stay at boarding school. There were boys his age there and sports. He liked football (he was on the team) and he was in the marching band. He wanted to play the trumpet, but the school councilor told him they already had enough trumpet players. Indians did best playing the base-drum, he said. Turns out, the counselor was right, Freddy was great on the base drum …but he had wanted to play the trumpet. He sort of got used to town living too, and then there were the girls. Girls became more important as the years went by. Freddy's mother knew then, that the pick-up truck was not enough.

Freddy had a girl when I met him, and sometimes I would see them walking down to the drugstore in the evening, kicking through the cottonwood leaves and holding hands. That was against the rules, but the government never caught them. The government was busy with Korea at the time and was letting a lot of things slide.

The drug store was the old-fashioned kind, with a soda fountain where you could order milk shakes and hamburgers, and play the Jukebox. The pharmacist was a nice old guy – he didn't care if the Indian kids came in, he treated them just like anybody else.

Freddy, and Francis (that was her name, Francis), would slip into the back booth and order cherry cokes and an order of fries. They would sit there and talk and laugh real low, the way Navajos do. Lots of times I would be in the booth next to them. I liked to listen to them talk Navajo. It sounded soft and gurgley ...like spring water. I used to wonder what they were talking about.

The government had used Navajos to relay secret messages during the second World War – It was one of the few codes the Germans never broke. Once I found that out, I didn't bother trying to learn the language anymore.

So now, twenty years later, here's Freddy and me, knocking back cold ones, and sort of sizing one another up. It had been ten years or so since I'd been back. He looked about the same. Indians don't change much in that amount of time. His hair was a little longer, but he wasn't queuing it up in back like some did. We had a couple of beers and talked for a while. He said he was working a few days a week at the new government housing project. "Disposal plant," he laughed, before I could ask. "It's o.k. I got a little place over there – those green ones.

You know, look like Monopoly houses," he laughed again. "But, only until the project's finished, then you have to be married to get one." He picked at the beer label with a furrowed brow. "They're damn sure not worth getting married for."

His mother was remarried and living over by Teec Nos Pos "At least I think she's married," he winked, "They still do a lot of things the old way over there. Hey! You remember me telling you about my little sister, Lilly? Well, she went all the way through college, got her degree and everything. Anthropology!"

"That's quite something!" I said, and I meant it too.

He looked out the front window "Yeah, it's hard to get a job right now though. BIAs not hiring. She's living over there with my mom until things turn loose." He took a long swallow of beer. "You should see her, wears her hair in a bun, velveteen blouse with long skirts, and plenty of silver and turquoise. All very traditional – looks like a hundred years ago. Goes around asking all the old people how it used to be, and writing it down in a notebook. The old people tell her too. They like her being dressed like that." He shook his head, "I don't see how any good can come of it. Those old times are gone, and writing it down in a book won't bring it back. But, what the hell, I guess that's what an anthropologist does," he shook his head again. "Whatever! I just don't see how any good can come of it." He turned around to watch the middle-aged barmaid turn a couple of quarters into music. "Play something good!" he called with a wave and a smile.

He finally got around to telling me what had happened with him and Francis. You've heard the story, they got married after high school, he worked off and on – she worked – he drank ...she got tired. She had left a long time ago. They had no children. "She went back to school. She's teaching down at Shiprock!" He said it with a sense of wonder, as though Francis had moved to New York and was working off-Broadway.

He got that old train-whistle-lonesome look on his face, "You know how it is man," he said, tapping the bottle in front of him, "it comes around and goes around. I can't complain; what the hell." Then he slapped me on the back and laughed, "I'd rather have a bottle in front of me than a frontal lobotomy!" He pointed to his cap – that's what it said on the front. Freddy was getting there! He had reached the bulletproof stage and I knew he was only about two beers short of a full load. He was beginning to fade fast; soon I wouldn't be able to see him anymore. I got the feeling he wouldn't want me around for that, so I stood up and put enough money on the bar for a couple more rounds. I didn't want Freddy to have to ask someone.

"Hey! If you get back through here, drop by my place. I'm in the government housing outside town ...those Monopoly houses – be happy to have you – anytime!"

I made a pistol of my thumb and forefinger and clicked it at him ...I do that sort of thing sometimes after a couple of beers.

Walking out of the bar, I could see the flagpole up at the dormitory on the hill. Old glory was whipping in the breeze. It looked good! It looked like it stood for something up there on the hill. Freddy owed the government a lot ...you might even say he owed 'em everything.

Fat of the Land

Las Rodillas

It was bound to happen
but who would
have thought

it would be the knees
that would be
first to go

that's what comes
of going through life
on your knees

Zapata had it right in
1911

Prefirio morir de pie
qué viver
de rodillas

I would rather die on my feet
than go on living
on my knees

Oil Field Trash

An old friend, I hadn't seen in many years, called the other night. Well, more than an old friend, really. We had gone through that mysterious "coming of age" together and had been inseparable.

"Hi, I'll bet you don't know who this is!" Slamming me back to one of America's little known frontiers.

He spoke in the same quiet, self-effacing manner I remembered, Okie accent barely discernible now. How many Okies must there be in California. I mean besides Steinbeck's Okies! I'm talking about the other Okies – the ones Steinbeck embarrassed. They hated him, you know, for what he made them out to be. "The Commie sonofabitch," they would say. I remember them still trickling through New Mexico in the late forties. Mattresses tied on old touring cars – dirty-faced young'uns with big eyes, hanging out the windows like tattered flags of the country they had left behind – heading for the Promised Land. I was a kid then myself, but I remember them all right.

They pulled into the old tourist court down the road, looking for a cheap place to wash off the dust and catch a few winks. Later, they would set out in front of the rooms in old orange metal lawn chairs, admiring the little strip of green grass, eating Spam sandwiches and drinking Delaware Punches. The kids were rangy, hard looking, road-weary ...leery, of anyone who had a house and a dog and a haircut. Okies!

I never saw one that wouldn't offer you a bite to eat though. I mean there were times I could see they didn't have enough to go around, but nothing would do them but you set down and have a little something. After they ate, the men would hitch up their bib-overalls and shamble out to the hi-way, squinting up the road into the sunset. Pushing back their sweat-stained hats, rubbing their white foreheads, they would look back at the women and say, "She ain't far now!" Hope was on the women then, you could see it in their hands – darting to a stray wisp of hair, smoothing a faded old house dress, ...they were ready.

After dark, the kids and I would shoot marbles or spin wooden tops in the flickering nuclear glow of the neon lights. One evening a tow-headed boy in torn overalls gave me a hand-carved top his grandpa had made for him, from a piece of mesquite root, back in Oklahoma. It was a work of art. The old man had known something about carving. When I said so, the boy looked at the top as though seeing it for the first time. He turned it over and over and I could see it well up inside him. Finally he just handed it back to me with that little half-way Okie grin. "My grandpa can make me another one," he said. When he went inside, another tow-head scrunched up her nose and whispered, "Our grandpa ain't gonna' make him no new one. Our grandpa's dead."

I didn't read Steinbeck until many years later of course – but he was right about the Okies – the pinko bastard.

My friend's voice, from his patio in California, was telling me about his new house. Apparently it had a pool. As I listened to him on the phone I thought: California! Swimming pools! That's not his world... or my world ...not the real world. We said all the things people say after twenty years, but they weren't the things we really wanted to say. The things we really wanted to say were locked up in a little boomtown in New Mexico back in the late fifties.

Trailer-houses were the only place available for folks like us back then. Not Mobile Homes, trailer houses, you could take them with you. If you had a good one it was maybe thirty feet long. That's a two bedroom, one of them more like a hallway really, with bunk beds. The living-room-kitchen was up front with a pullout couch that could be made into yet another bed in about twelve seconds. A family of five or six could live quite comfortably there ...if they didn't know any better.

People came from all over, from oil fields they had already drilled out, pumped down, or run dry. Okies and Texans mostly, though you might find people from most anywhere. Like all boom towns it had its share of the drifters and trouble makers, who for lack of a better way to waste their lives, followed the oil patch. But there were regular hard working people too. Years later, they joked, calling themselves Oil-Field Trash, flaunting bumper-stickers that said OIL FIELD TRASH AND PROUD OF IT. Back then they didn't say that, they knew who they were, and what they were – they didn't need any bumper-stickers to remind them.

The little town fairly pulsed with excitement, brimming over with the energy and greed that comes with oil and gas. I know it may be hard to picture if you are not from around there, so I'd like to get it exactly right. If you can visualize a gambling casino, filled with desperately poor people, who can't afford NOT to be there – that would be close.

There was the wildest assortment imaginable. Geologists and engineers from back east, wheeler dealers from the big oil companies, farmers and cowboys and Mexicans, and being on the edge of the largest Indian reservation in the world, there were plenty of those too …Navajos mostly. Everyone was a closet ethnologist and spent a lot of time trying to figure out who was what and where from. They thought it might give them a survivalist's edge; not a bad idea where people tend to live on the cusp, with violence and outrage never more than a heartbeat away. The town ran wide open, with bars that started early and sold beer and trouble by the case. Fistfights broke out at the drop of an innuendo and cars and pickup trucks went roaring up and down the streets until the wee hours of the morning. Drunk driving was considered a recreational device and the roughnecks wagered their lives on a daily basis.

A woman... stabbed her husband to death right in front of the bar on the corner of first and main; at the only traffic light in town. They had just come out, and were standing there in the bright daylight, arguing, and waiting for the light to change. It was red. The man couldn't see it very well and was shading his eyes with his hand. She grew louder, and began emphasizing her point by poking him in the chest. With a ten-inch butcher knife. Apparently, she managed to put forth a pretty convincing argument because he was dead when he hit the sidewalk, just as the traffic light turned green and said GO ...and he did. That was the last traffic light he ever had to wait on. The bloodstain became part of the cement and part of our lives too. For weeks we would see it every day on our way home from school. We didn't have to go home that way, of course, but it was only about a block out of the way, little enough trouble to see where a man had ended his life and a woman had started a new one of a whole different sort. That stain is still there, I saw it only recently, though there's no way it could have lasted this long.

I hope you don't get the impression that we lived in terror, or that this type of thing cast any sort of shadow on our childhood, because it didn't ...that I'm aware of. We grew up in this sort of atmosphere, and you must understand, that to us, it was just a normal part of life and we didn't dwell on it to any great extent. In the evening, at suppertime, when the hustle and bustle died down, it was a pretty little town with quiet side streets shaded by giant cottonwood trees. You could see that it might have been a pleasant place to whittle away twenty or thirty years of your life ...before the oil field came in.

As you might imagine, there were the usual people that stand out in such a place. One of them was "Sonny." I never knew his real name but every small town has one – the town character if you will. I would judge him to be about thirty years old at the time, though it's hard to say. The years don't seem to weigh quite as heavy on folks like Sonny, lack of stress maybe. He had the mental ability of a child and roamed at will, knew everyone and was well liked. I can't ever remember him being ridiculed or ill-used, which you might have thought would be the case, considering the time and place. He dressed in bib-overalls, rolled up to fit, and a policeman's hat. I suppose it could have been a service station hat too, like the Texaco man wore...who knows, the thing was, Sonny thought it was a policeman's hat.

He was slightly hare-lipped and always had the stub end of a cigar in his mouth, and football was his passion. Not the game so much, I guess, but rather the crowd and the band and the feel of everyone being together, being part of something. He never missed a game. I can still see him down on the sidelines marching back and forth directing traffic; acting worried when we were in trouble, and helping with the cheers when things were going well. Late arrivals passing by would ask the score and always he answered the same, "Nine to four, boy, nine to four!" He never deviated from these figures and it became a form of greeting between him and the townspeople wherever they might meet. "What's the score, Sonny?"

"Nine to four, boy – nine to four!"

Sonny and the person asking would part company equally comforted by the fact that someone, at least, still knew the score.

You're probably wondering how Sonny fits in with all this. Well he doesn't really, no more than he fit in anywhere else. Years later, when his mother died, they took him away to the state home, where eventually he came to believe himself invisible, and so, of course, after a time he will be. Already his name has disappeared. I would just like for you to think he was part of this story... I know he did.

Of course there is always a girl, and this one was a wonderfully warmhearted, bright and funny girl. The finest kind of girl really. Sometimes she and I would sort of hang around together. I mean, we didn't date or anything – we knew that wasn't what we were about. Oh we might go down to the soda fountain after school, and then later I might walk her home. She was uncannily attuned to my innermost thoughts and with the most delectable sense of humor. By the time we arrived we would be laughing so hard we had to lean against the trees in her front yard. She pretended she didn't care that we didn't go out. I know she did care though. I knew it then too, and felt badly for us both. My regular girlfriend in a nearby town was pretty and pretentious, and without a brain in her head. I cringe now to think of the time I wasted on her (and it was wasted). I could have been with that other girl and it's her I think of now when I remember those days. How could I have know how rare someone like that would be. I hope she found someone who knew what she was really worth. We used to do some things, back then, my friend and I, things that kids wouldn't think of doing today. They were the kind of things that wouldn't make sense anymore.

We drove a 1930 Model A Ford, a two-door sedan with the top chopped off and nearly twice as old as we were. For the same amount of money we could have had a bull-nosed '49 Ford coupe with a flathead V-8 and a heater. Now that would have made sense and it would have made the winters pass more quickly too. But that Model A …it was fire engine red, with a stick shift on the floor and a windshield you could crank out for ventilation. That seemed like a plus when we bought it that summer. We liked to think it was the kind of car John Dillinger might have driven. Actually, it looked exactly like the one in the "Archie" comic books and the girls were crazy about it …in warm weather.

The previous owner had been a fifty-five year old high school football coach from a neighboring town, who could actually remember those cars when they were brand new. He drove it to school each morning ...foxtail flying from the aerial, his old letter jacket flapping in the breeze ...a song in his heart. Apparently, for him, the car was part of some elaborate ritual, possibly brought on by an early male menopause. He loved that car, and when I came to look at it he told me he wouldn't think of selling it, except that his wife of twenty years had suddenly left him, taking their real car and all the money he had in the world. With winter coming on he was forced, at last, to face reality. "Sonofbitch," he said ...he just wasn't as young as he used to be.

Model A's weren't considered collector cars at the time, there were too many of them lying around in wrecking yards and old barns, which was a good thing, because as it turned out, those were the only parts supply available. The owners of the derelict cars, however, wouldn't sell pieces. They were waiting for the cars to become more valuable, something they felt was inevitable. That's when they would make a real killing, they said. Poor attitude, we thought, but it posed purely theoretical objections, as we had no money for parts anyway.

It was the old Midnight Auto Supply for the likes of us. We didn't feel it any more wrong than say, swiping watermelons. We felt God made those watermelons for all his children, not just his children with money. I forget exactly how we extrapolated this theory over to the Model A parts, but it made perfect sense at the time. Even the Baptist preacher's son went on watermelon raids with us, which was a great comfort. We felt that if God struck anyone dead it would surely be him. We came to regard him as a kind of human lightning rod and were absolutely fearless when he was along. Unfortunately, we could never interest him in auto parts, as he had no car ...and he seldom rode around with us in the daytime. He was a heavy-set boy with a pleasant face and later became quite popular in our senior year – at which time he refused to have any further to do with us. It was in his best interest I'm sure, and was no more than we deserved, we being the way we were and all.

... "Yes! ...Yes! If you ever get out this way be sure and drop by... We'll have a few beers. like old times ...of course, bring the family, they'll love it here - there's the pool." His voice was growing fainter. I could feel him fading away among the orange groves and almond trees. He had said all he could say and I knew he was anxious now to hang up, to move along to whatever they do on a summer afternoon out there, cocktails around the pool, an impending barbeque perhaps. There would be friends coming over, new friends, who wouldn't be interested in things that happened star years ago in another galaxy.

No matter, those were the real days of our lives. I wish we'd had some inkling then, of their far-reaching effect. Not that we could have done them differently or would want to go back and do them over. We already did them the best we knew how ...we did them the best we could.

R. Allen Chappell

The Secret

Here's an old man
70 ...maybe 75 years old
on his uppers
a wino maybe

and he's telling me
he knows
the secret of life
...I don't say nothing

it's easy, he says
taking another pull
at a brown
paper bag

life keeps
knocking you down
and you, just keep
getting back up

when you quit getting up
it's over
we're talking bare bones here
just the basics

...but by God
I think he's
on to something

Best in the West

New Mexico – the Enchanted Land, where mesas, canyons and sky all run together like something out of the Old Testament and the relentless wind and sun conspire in their endless carving of sand, and rock, and people. The sun! Lord ...how can I tell you about the sun? Unless you've chopped cotton, or bucked bales, at 104° there's really no way for you to understand.

It's all mechanized now of course, but it was Mexicanized then. Dollar twenty-five an hour, ten hours a day and six days a week – good money for the time and place, what with gasoline at twenty-five cents a gallon and a cheeseburger and chocolate shake for a dollar. If you could stick it out for three weeks you could buy a pretty good used car, even after the deductions. Those deductions... Mr. Garcia swore they were right, but he never asked us for a social-security number or anything. I don't think the Government ever saw those deductions. We pretty much figured we were just working for a dollar an hour and let it go at that. I don't blame Mr. Garcia now – the same had been done to him for years – he was just trying to get **his** deductions back.

Mr. Garcia was the first Mexican I'd known to start his own business – hay contracting – had a tractor-trailer rig and everything. I had a lot of respect for that. It was something you didn't see every day. I always called him Mr. Garcia instead of Hector like the other guys ...those railroad tracks were a hard thing to cross back then.

On Sundays when the rest of the crew had the day off, Mr. Garcia would pull that big old Mack up in the yard and start polishing it. His oldest boy, Robert, would be underneath changing the oil and the youngest son, Abe, would be up in the engine compartment checking the fluids and so on. Robert was a first string quarterback for our senior line-up and it was said that he had real potential. Mr. Garcia talked a lot about Robert going to college.

The truck was candy-apple red and not more than eight or nine years old – you'd have thought it was a new one, if you didn't know anything about trucks. And there weren't any fuzzy dice hanging off the mirror or little plastic Jesus on the dashboard either. It was a business truck, he said, he was a businessman. They would work on it all day long, so it would look good on Monday, when they hauled the hay to the dairies in Amarillo. The Garcia's were really proud of that truck. Mr. Garcia's daughter, Mimi, who took art, painted signs on the doors – GARCIA & SONS TRUCKING – bold white letters outlined in black and silver to match the wheels. For a while there had been some smaller print that said "Best in the West" but Mr. Garcia thought it sounded too uppity and had her paint over it.

When I signed on to work, Mr. Garcia said I wouldn't last two weeks. He was right too, on the tenth day, with the temperature hovering around 104 degrees; I passed out on top of a Semi-load of hay and fell all the way to the ground. I say 'all the way to the ground' because I want you to know how far it was. I didn't wake up for over an hour. Mr. Garcia and Robert were dripping cold water from a canvas bag onto my forehead. The canvas bag had a picture of a camel on it. Funny I should remember that after all these years, but I can see that camel like it was yesterday. Mr. Garcia was really happy to see me open my eyes and said I should take the rest of the day off and stay out of the sun. Robert told me, in private, that he thought I should just quit. He said he didn't think white kids were geared for that kind of work and maybe I should find a different sort of job in town. He didn't mean anything by it he said – just that he thought maybe the sun was too much for a "light complected' kid like me.

When I went by for my check, Mr. Garcia invited me in to eat, as he often would, and I did because I love Mexican food. Mrs. Garcia was known to set a great table. She had out-done herself this time, with ranchero style enchiladas filled with roast cabrito and covered in a rich, dark chili sauce, the kind made from the sweet, wrinkled-black Pasillas she raised in the back yard. It was all served bubbly hot with lots of melted longhorn cheese. There were side dishes of Spanish rice and real Mexican *frijjoles*, those that simmer with a piece of salt pork on the back of the stove for two days, before being refried and sprinkled with white goat cheese. Of course there were baskets of big, floppy hot, flour tortillas wrapped in white towels. I grew up on Mexican food and have eaten it all over, but I still judge them all by Mrs. Garcia's cooking. She and Mimi later opened a Mexican restaurant right there in the house and people came clear from San Jon to eat – it was that good. Those Garcia's were born business people.

After dinner Mr. Garcia got out his tally book and figured up my hours, took out for the deductions and all, then told me I had been a good worker and lasted longer than he expected. He smiled, and said I could work for him anytime. Those were fine words coming from him. Mr. Garcia didn't say anything he didn't mean. When it came time to leave, Mimi followed me out to the front gate. She said I shouldn't feel bad about passing out and falling off the truck... me being so 'light complected' and all.

Summer was nearly over, and I needed a job that would fit in with school, so I didn't go back to work for the Garcias. Instead, through some wry twist of fate, I fell into a job as a radio announcer at the local station. Strange how your fortunes can change so quickly when you are young and have no real measure of life. It was the only radio station in nearly 100 miles – 250 watts of radiated power – about the same as a big light bulb. Sometimes our old transmitter would barely push our voices out past the town limits, but no matter, beyond that we were mostly just covering Jackrabbits anyway. I used to think a lot about those Jackrabbits sitting out there on the prairie turning this way and that, their long ears trying to pick up a little "Shotgun Boogie" or maybe doing a little furry-footed shuffle to Louie Armstrong's "Muskrat Ramble."

The studio (and I use the term loosely) sat right on the hi-way at the edge of town. There was a large picture window looking out on the road and I could watch the traffic go by during records. The Garcia's quickly became my biggest fans and would slow the truck way down on their way by the station to catch me doing a live commercial. They would honk the air-horn furiously, which of course came across on the air. They never tired of hearing their truck on the radio and seemed to get such a kick out of it that I didn't have the heart to say anything. I always dedicated the next song to "Garcia And Sons Trucking Co." I kept a copy of Eddy Arnold's "Cattle Call" handy, as I knew this was Mr. Garcia's favorite. He would always tune in the noonday livestock report just to hear the intro music, which was that. On their way back into town they would toot the air horn again and I would look up to see them laughing and waving. I can still see Robert leaning across his father to give me the thumbs up sign.

Five kids in our senior class were killed in car wrecks that year and Robert was one of them. Mr. Garcia was never really the same afterwards, and the next year, sold the truck to a feedlot. Abe joined the army and Mimi got married and moved to Albuquerque. Mr. Garcia began staying around home a lot, helping with the restaurant and drinking a little whisky.

A few months after the accident there had been a letter from New Mexico Western offering Robert a football scholarship. They say Mr. Garcia would take that letter out in the evenings and read it over and over. I attended New Mexico Western myself that year, though not on a scholarship. When I came home for a visit that first month, Mr. Garcia asked me how the football team was shaping up. I told him they hadn't done too well in practice games and that we could only hope for the best. He shook his head and unfolded Robert's scholarship letter from his old trucker's wallet and passed it across to me. I acted like it was the first I had heard of it. He sighed and told me what a shame it was that Robert wasn't our quarterback ...might have made all the difference.

New Mexico Western lost every single game that year.

Last summer, passing through that country, I noticed an old Mack truck sitting abandoned in a field outside town. It was just the cab and chassis, the paint faded to a chalky orange and weeds growing up through the frame. I pulled off and walked over to make sure... and that was it all right. The windshield was broken out and the upholstery full of rats nests, but on the right hand door you could still make out GARCIA AND SONS TRUCKING ...and just beneath that, where the cover paint had peeled away, were the still bright letters, "Best In The West."

When You're Hot

"You're a writer? You sure don't look like a writer," the drunk offered, steadying himself with the bar rail – the Great Wallenda, with a brass balancing pole. "By God ...I'm fifty three years old ...cowboy'd, ...roughneck'd, ...spent four years on freighters out of Frisco," he belched, "I could tell you some things to write about sport!" He was trying to find his mouth with his beer, using the mirror behind the bar as a teleprompter. "Yer damn right I could tell ya'. Things you won't see in your lifetime Ace!"

I moved down a stool. I've been around drunks all my life and I tire of them rather quickly now.

"Hey pardner," he said reaching for my arm, "I didn't mean nothin' by it. Hell, buy me a drink ...we'll forget the whole deal," he laughed, a rough, gravelly sound with no humor in it. I was just out of range now, he didn't trust himself to let go of the bar rail. He was working without a net and he knew it.

I hadn't been talking to him in the first place. I'd been talking to the blonde woman on my right. I was just trying to make conversation, you know, pass the time.

She was no looker I can tell you, painfully thin, and too much make-up. She seemed nervous, giggled a lot, like maybe she shouldn't be there. The town only had one bar. It was called the Silver Dilly ...I didn't ask. It wasn't what I'd call a going concern. There were only four customers scattered around, not counting the drunk, the blonde and myself. No one was smoking – it could have been a Mormon bar. Maybe they were all Jack-Mormons.

It was the middle of the afternoon, hot and muggy even with the air conditioner going. If you've been in that country in July, after the rains, you know what I mean. A middle-aged Navajo couple was sitting at a table up front by the window, sucking on Budweiser longnecks and keeping an eye on their pickup truck, which had the back end full of groceries. I remember hoping they didn't have any ice cream out there.

I had been heading for Flagstaff when the radiator hose busted. I couldn't believe my luck, I mean it was bad luck to lose the hose, but lucky it happened right at the top of the hill outside town. I took the old pickup out of gear and she coasted right into the Chevron station. The attendant – one of those new age Indian kids – spoke English with absolutely no sign of an accent. That's something that's still hard for me to get used too. He rummaged around in the back room for a while but couldn't come up with the exact hose, so he called the next town over to have one sent down on the evening bus. The kid went out of his way to be nice. Something else I have a hard time with. I hoped he wouldn't put a smiley face on my bill. I had a couple of hours to kill and that's how I wound up at the Silver Dilly. It just goes to show how fate works sometimes.

The two other customers were a hippy-looking cow-boy with long hair, asleep in a booth, drooling on his arm. And a short, bulldozer-built Mexican at a back ta-ble, next to the jukebox. It was the Mexican that caught my eye – flat headed as a catfish – with the long stringy mustaches to go with it. He fiddled with a sweaty mug of draft as though it were a piece of bait he couldn't quite figure out. Every now and then he would look at the door, as though expecting someone long past due. He looked like he could be a "bad hombre" as Louie L'amour might say.

The bartender was one of those rare no-talkers that just become invisible after a while, the worst possible kind for a bar business. People would stay home and drink if booze was all they wanted. The blonde was mak-ing up for it though, with the kind of mindless, giggling, prattle that allows you to think about other things and still hold up your end of the conversation. She had just gotten a divorce ...moved here to lose an insanely jealous ex-husband. Well, she had picked the right place ...it was about as lost as you could get. She worked at the curio shop-cafe across the street and hoped to wind up in Phoenix by fall. The heat there would kill you right now, she said.

"So, you're a writer, huh? You mean like Stephen King? I read one of his books... scary as hell!"

"Well, not exactly like Stephen King." I admitted, "I don't write anything scary ...and I'm not published; but, other than that ...yeah, I guess you could say I'm like him."

"Oh, well, hey, don't let it get you down. We all have to start somewhere. Look at me! I'm starting over. I'm signed up for cosmetology school this fall. I mean...you can't let it get you down ...right?"

She was absolutely right of course, out of the mouths of babes... You can't let it get you down.

The drunk had begun edging his way down the bar toward us, in that meticulously casual manner drunks have when trying to appear sober. He wanted either another drink, or the blonde, or... a fight. He wouldn't pose much of a threat in any of the three, but I kept an eye on him anyway. It's the quiet drunks you have to watch. The blonde noticed too, and suggested we go sit at a table.

The drunk remained, staring in the mirror, a sad little look on his face; he couldn't believe we would be so rude. There was no way he could make it over to that table. It was as though we had moved across the Grand Canyon. He knew he would have to be the Evil Kneviel of all drunks to make it to that table.

The Mexican was staring at us now. There was just the hint of a little smile hanging from the ends of his mustache, like a bent trapeze. I didn't think anything of it at the time; but I would come to look back upon it as one of the great, misinterpreted signals of my life.

We had another round; talking about ...I don't remember what. She said she had a mobile home over behind the cafe and I should come over—rest up until my pickup was fixed. She said she had to leave pretty soon anyway, to change for work; it was a split shift. I was mulling this over ...when the door busted open, slamming into the Indian couple's table, and causing the man to chip a tooth on the longneck. He exclaimed loudly in Navajo. There are virtually no curse words in that tongue. I've often wondered what he said.

Silhouetted in the glare was the biggest human in a hard-hat I'd ever seen. I heard the blonde suck in her breath so hard it sounded like the airbrakes on a Freightliner. I instantly knew the whole story, as though I had just seen a movie based on her life. It was a movie I didn't want, even a minor role in. I hit the ground running for the back of the bar where, instinctively, I hoped I would find restrooms, with windows leading to safety and a new chance at life.

"Get him Chewy!" came a bellow from the doorway and the Mexican came unbolted from his chair like a two hundred pound Channel Cat with a double-ought hook in his mouth ...I knew who he'd been waiting for now. Chewy had obviously played some football and had me figured for an end run. Fear, however, had given me wings and he was not quite set when I hit him full in the face, elbow first. It was the same sensation I'd felt running into a large tree as a child – unless you've done it, I can't tell you how much it hurts.

Behind me, I could hear the big man coming down the bar with a roar. The Mexican's nose was squirting blood – a good sign – there's not a man in the world that does well with a broken nose, believe me when I tell you this. As I sidestepped Chewy's flailing arms, there was a tremendous crash behind me and I realized that the big man had gone down. I found later that it was the drunk that had stuck his foot out. What spark of human kindness inspired him I can't say – perhaps he did it instinctively ...rotten to the core. Whatever the reason, I will always wish good things for him.

I hit the bathroom door, and found all as it should be; the window open, to pull the draft from the air-conditioner and the commode just the right height for getting through the window As the song says: "When you're hot you're hot."

When the blonde returned to her trailer I was having a baloney sandwich and soaking my elbow in cold water in the kitchen sink. "I figured you might be here," she said giggling, "There's not that many places to hide." She sat down in a kitchen chair and wiped her face with a dishtowel "Well the State Police got Charlie ...and he got a broken arm when he fell, too." She giggled abruptly, and then grew thoughtful. "That Chewy got away ...but I don't expect he'll be back." She fanned herself with the towel. "It sure is hot." There were little beads of perspiration on her upper lip and her mascara was a mess. "Oh! Jimmy over at the station had to head home but he said your truck's ready. He sure thinks you're lucky, having that hose blow out so close to town. ...And he said to have a nice day too.

R. Allen Chappell

In Retrospect

He's 48 years old and his life
is beginning to thin out around him
like river ice in springtime

nothing he can put his finger on
just a vague brittleness
that hadn't been there before

time for a Porsche
and designer jeans
not in this lifetime he smiles

more like the porch and pork and beans.
children call …California dreamin'
You should come out here they say

this is where the people are
it makes him stop and wonder
he thinks of all the money he's spent

on whiskey and women
it was a lot …and he's glad
he didn't just waste it

Beechal Mercury *(as the banana king 1949)*

The store-man, adjusting his spectacles, peered over the massive wooden counter at my friend's small black face. "What's your name boy?" he asked in a wrinkled old voice.

"Beechal Mercury," my friend replied immediately, causing me to jump back a little. I wouldn't have gone with him if I had known it would come to this. Oh, he often used assumed names – seeming to prefer nearly anything to Hershel Leroy Hunnicut. That was his real name. He would make up names on the spur of the moment, pulling them out of his nappy head as a magician pulls rabbits out of a hat. It was frightening really to see an eight year old with such presence of mind and I never ceased to wonder at it.

The old man raised his stubbly chin and looked at us through the bottom half of his glasses, thoughtfully wiping his hands on his dirty white apron. "That's a mighty peculiar name boy." he said testily, "I don't believe I know any Mercurys around here."

"Yas'ur, well that's my name alright. That's the name my momma give me alright."

I could not have been more mortified, I mean lying about your name was one thing, but dragging your momma into it was way beyond what I was used to.

"...Un-huh" the grocer said pursing his lips and nodding his head as though it all made sense now. "Beechal Mercury huh, well what can I do for you Beechal?"

Beechal glanced back at me for a moment, "We wants five dollars worth of bananas," he said to the store-man, coming right out with it.

Now it was the store-man's turn to jump back a little. "Five dollars worth of bananas is a good many bananas Beechal," he said, indicating a sign over the produce counter behind us. We both turned to look at the sign, a hand-drawn picture of a yellow banana with the price underneath. The price was 10¢ which we could read though we were unfamiliar with the per lb. notation that followed. "I calculate, off-hand, that five dollars would buy an entire stalk of bananas weighing over fifty pounds. 'Course I always take off for the stalk," he assured us. "Are you boys sure your mommas want fifty pounds of bananas?

"Oh, I expect it will take at least that many," Beechal said adamantly, turning to me, nodding for verification. "His momma is making banana cakes for the church picnic. She says to us ...she says, 'Now you boys be sure and fetch a full five dollars worth of bananas, cause my banana cakes go fast at the church picnic.'

This was the worst kind of lie as my momma had told us nothing of the sort and had never made a banana cake in her life, to my knowledge. There was nothing for it now however, it was madness, but I was in too deep and began lying frantically in support of Beechal's every word (I thought of him as "Beechal" myself now.)

"We'll need every bit of fifty pounds," I confirmed ...Beechal and I nodding furiously in unison.

"How do you intend to get fifty pounds of bananas home," the store-man inquired, tapping his fingers on the counter, looking intently from one to the other of us. "We don't deliver."

"Oh, no sir, we know that. Don't we know that." Beechal grinned at me. "We got's his wagon outside." It was true; my Radio Flyer was parked just outside the door. One thing Beechal and I had in common was ...bananas! We loved them – no, that's not the right word – we craved them. We craved bananas like some folks crave strong drink or religion.

Beechal's daddy ran a pool-hall down on First Street and sometimes we would drop by after school and Chug would bring us out a Delaware Punch. We were not allowed inside. Chug Hunnicut was small – skinny like Beechal – and wore a broad brimmed hat and flashy ties. He and Beechal's momma were separated and Lidia did ironing for my momma every Thursday afternoon. Thursday, being the day after washday at our house. Having the ironing done was one of the few luxuries my momma afforded herself, though lord knows where she came up with the money for it each week. (five dollars being a lot of money in those days)

That's what Beechal had said just that morning. "Five dollars is a lot of money," he noted, sitting out on the porch steps, pondering our itinerary for the day. "Yo momma got's five dollars in there on the table." (in those days "Yo momma" was a legitimate term, often used when referring to someone's mother)

"How many bananas you reckon you could buy with five dollars?" Beechal wondered, going snake-eyed at the prospect.

"I expect that five dollars is for the ironing," I reminded him, knowing Beechal was fully aware of it. My momma always laid Lidia's five dollars out in plain view as sort of an incentive I suppose – or perhaps as proof of our ability to pay. In any case the bill would lie there until the ironing was finished, at which time my momma would perform the small ceremony of handing over the money while exclaiming hugely over the amount of work Lidia had accomplished. Lidia, smiling her big wide smile would wave her hand as though shooing flies, "What? That little old bit of ironing?" she would say, "They ain't no need for this kind of money for that little dab a clothes," all the while pretending to push the money away. She would take it in the end of course ...both women laughing together at their own good fortune.

Beechal had fallen into a contemplative frame of mind which I knew concerned the five dollars and possibly bananas. It was going to be a long, hot, day and the thought of what Beechal might have in mind was causing me to break out in a premature sweat.

"I believe I know a way we can make a little money for our ownselves today," Beechal declared. "They ain't no need in that five dollars just laying around the house all day when it could be out working, making something of itself, so to speak." This was a term I had heard Chug use on various occasions and I noted it as a cautionary resemblance between father and son.

The plan, in basic terms, was to buy a large, as yet unknown, quantity of bananas and take them around the neighborhood, selling them door to door for as yet an undetermined amount of profit, which we would split between us after replacing the original five dollars.

There would of course be a superfluous number of bananas to spare, which would be available to the two of us on an unlimited basis. The money would be just a loan Beechal assured me. We would have plenty of time to replace it before four o'clock. "Moderately optimistic" would be the best description of my attitude to the proposal, as I had seen several of Beechal's plans work quite well in the past, though nothing of this magnitude I can assure you.

The store-man provided several burlap bags to be used as padding in the wagon, and at the last minute whipped a damp burlap off a bin of cabbages to provide a sun shield for the load. "Now you watch those bumps," he cautioned as we eased the wagon out on to the sidewalk.

Beechal, being barefoot, felt that he should have the more desirable job of steering while I, who wore tennis shoes, would be of greater service attached to the back of the wagon, providing brakes as it were, on the long downhill run. As luck would have it there was just enough room in front of the bananas for Beechal to sit, though the wagon-tongue was nearly vertical and offered limited control at best. I warned Beechal that this mode of steering could be dangerous and that I would be happy to lend him my shoes and take the front position myself. But he wouldn't hear of it, assuring me that he had much experience in this sort of thing and was quite capable of handling it himself. I remember grumbling under my breath at the prospect of walking while he again rode. Beechal, being an extraordinary manipulator of human beings, reached up and broke off a banana which he passed back to me smiling in a most conciliatory manner. After choosing a banana for himself, He motioned me underway, each of us, now with a fruit in one hand and our fate in the other.

We had gone only a short distance when Beechal, whose mouth was full, began signaling for me to slow down. I could see that he was having difficulty steering with one hand, as was I holding back the wagon. He quickly stuffed the rest of the banana into his mouth, regrettably, letting the peel fall to the sidewalk, as he took to his task in earnest. The last thing I remember after stepping on that banana peel was the whites of Beechal's eyes as he looked around to see what had become of the brakes. Lying flat on my stomach on that sidewalk, watching Beechal on a roller-coaster ride to hell, I knew once again that life was unquestionably good and just.

Though I feared greatly for the safety of my Radio Flyer, I knew that its fate was in as capable and concerned hands as possible – there was little else to be done on my end. Catching up with the fleeing wagon was out of the question. By the time I could gather my wits and pick myself up, Beechal was traveling at an extraordinary rate of speed for that particular model of wagon. It occurred to me that when Beechal reached the cross street at the bottom of the hill it would be necessary for him to leave the sidewalk by way of a six inch curb, a move I considered iffy at best. This accomplished, however, it would be smooth sailing, in a manner of speaking, across the street and right up a steeply inclined driveway, which gave every indication of being the answer to both our prayers. I still feel this is exactly what might have taken place too, if it hadn't been for eighty-four year old Rose

Shufflemyre, who happened to be out for a drive in her red, 1949, Pontiac Chieftain.

The particulars of what was to follow were so indelibly imprinted on my mind that I can to this day visualize them in the most minute detail. The Pontiac appeared as if from nowhere, though Miss Rose seldom traveled over twenty miles an hour and was a meticulous driver. Even at that distance I could see Beechal turning his head in recognition of this added danger, the whites of his eyes clearly discernible, cheeks still distended with banana, terror plainly written on every feature. Even as he became air-borne from the curb I could see that Miss Rose, with remarkable alertness for one of her years, had begun applying the brakes; probably the worst thing she could have done under the circumstances. I still believe Beechal would have missed the Pontiac entirely had she just continued on at her original rate of speed. That not being the case, however, Beechal and my wagon struck the rear quarter panel of the Chieftain while still in mid-flight, erupting in a spectacular shower of bananas and wagon parts. Once again, in an instantaneous revelation, the vagaries of fate had been made clear to me and I could plainly see how tenuous and fragile our positions in life really are. As I raced downhill toward the scene of the accident, my mind was a turmoil of extraneous facts and fancies each vying to shut out the crush of reality. I focused on the chrome hood ornament of the automobile, a likeness of an Indian chieftain's head complete with flowing red plastic head dress, which was rumored to be electrically illuminated by a small bulb when the headlights were turned on – a report we could never verify as Miss Rose did not drive at night.

Tearing my attention from the hood ornament, I became aware of Beechal lying amid the wreckage of bananas and wagon. There was no mark on him that I could discern and as I drew closer his soft moans assured me that he was still alive, though that possibility had not crossed my mind. Miss Rose, amazingly spry, for one of such age, (adrenalin rush or not) was making her way around the off side of the car. Beechal, with my help, was sitting up now, rubbing his head, though as I have said there was no mark of any kind. He solemnly surveyed what was left of our business venture all the while moaning softly to himself. Suddenly, as he saw Miss Rose coming around the rear of the car, he swooned backwards into my arms with the most pitiable of sounds.

"Are you O. K. Beechal?" I asked in a voice too low for Miss Rose to hear. He opened one eye slightly and gritted his teeth at me in a way I took to mean he was alright.

"Try to get five dollars," he whispered between clinched teeth. I knew instinctively what he was getting at and rolled my eyes upward for strength.

Miss Rose was watching us intently now with her little bird eyes not missing a trick. "Is that boy going to be alright," she inquired sharply. Any thoughts I had of expounding upon the vast implications of running over... were immediately squashed.

"Well, yes mam ...I mean I think he will be ...unless there's internal injuries ...something we can't see," I was certain Miss Rose could see I was no doctor, but the effort to define the situation had to be made. Beechal moaned extra loud at this.

"Humph!" she said,"I guess you had better put him in the car and let me drive him over to the emergency room."

Beechal sat straight up at this and looked around as though in a daze. "Where am I?" he asked in a loud voice.

"You been run over Beechal," I said, knowing it was not true in the strictest sense.

"Did all the bananas get runned over too?" he asked looking around as though for the first time.

"Some of 'em did." I allowed, "And the rest of them aren't too good."

"Well, I guess that's the end of it then." Beechal said, tears welling up in his eyes for the first time. "My momma's gonna beat me for sure now." This was probably true enough, and me right along with him. I felt the hot tears of remorse in my own eyes at the very thought of it.

"Do you want to go to the hospital boy?" Miss Rose insisted more gently. "If you do, I'll take you over there right now." She was looking in wonder at the great profusion of bananas lying about in various stages of corruption.

"No 'um," Beechal declined in a weak voice, "I don't reckon I need the hospital," he surveyed the wreckage, "not just yet anyhow." He shook his head sadly. "The bananas is gone... the five dollars is gone..." he turned to me, "Yo wagon is gone," as though I might not have noticed. "I expects we'll get the beating of our life's today."

Miss Rose was fingering the dented quarter panel of her Pontiac. "I hope my insurance man understands about this," she murmured smiling at us for the first time. "He wasn't too happy last time,"

"We ain't got no insurance," Beechal stated absent-mindedly, and to no one in particular.

"No I don't imagine you do," Miss Rose agreed thoughtfully, taking off her eyeglasses and wiping them on a frilly white handkerchief. "What do you suppose your damages amount to? ...And don't you boys lie to me now," waggling her finger.

Beechal quickly looked at me, and then back to Miss Rose, "Well, there's the bananas of course," he said indicating what was left of them with a sweeping gesture. "...And then there's this wagon," he noted almost as an afterthought, making a little half-hearted kick in its direction.

"It was nearly new!" I put in hopefully, praying something good might come of all this.

"Yes, well, I expect that my son Marvin down at the garage can fix that wagon in short order. You take it down there and tell him I said so." She began digging around in a large patent leather purse which she had hung on one arm. "...And in regard to these bananas..." she said shaking her head, "I believe I heard five dollars mentioned?"

"Yes 'um," we answered together, anticipation now lapping at the shores of a great sea of hopelessness.

She extracted a rumpled five-dollar bill from her purse handing it to Beechal without ceremony. "See that this gets back to your mother," she said, turning to leave. As she reached the front of the car she looked back at us and said cryptically, "The best laid plans of mice and men *gang aft aglae.*"

Beechal and I thought about this for a time, but could make no sense of it, as neither of us had been to Scotland and were unaware of the connotation. After Miss Rose drove off in her dented Pontiac, Beechal looked at me and then at the bananas "Let's see how many a these suckers we can sell 'fore they turns bad!"

New York Book Review

These poets, as they call themselves,
trust me, most are only typists
unborn in wombs of academia
drunk on books and cerebral devices

they agonize and proselytize
in pseudo-intellectual meanderings
so codified only other academicians
can grasp their savant philandering

...give me old Vess Quinlan
or J.B. Allen when he's right
you'll see just how the common man
creates uncommon clarity and light

fifty years from now will tell us
which has stayed the storm
who's been buried by the way
in shrouds of literary form

Sour grapes oh lout! You say?
...completely plausible description
I'm just glad I read it free
and not by paid subscription.

The Llano

In April of the year Ella May Fossie turned thirty-four years old, there came word from the railroad telegraph office, twenty miles to the south, that a small band of Indians had walked away from their incarceration at Bosque Redondo. Government trackers followed them a good distance before losing their trail, but felt pretty certain the renegades would continue on in a northeasterly direction. It was thought they were trying to reach the Territory, where they might lose themselves among the many tribes of the Indian Nations.

The news would not ordinarily have been cause for any great concern, except that five of the seven were Apache. Three Jicarilla, and two Mescalero; one of the latter being the notorious Johnny Hat, so villainous, his own tribe would have nothing more to do with him. To be sure, all seven had reputations, including the two Navajo, who do not ordinarily fall into the same category when it comes to this sort of thing. Johnny Hat, however, was considered to be of the greatest concern.

When news of the escape reached the Fossie ranch, Frank Teal, who had brought the message, along with the monthly supplies, made it sound as ominous as possible; though secretly he thought any danger well past, as the

Indians should already have been beyond them, the message then being a number of days old.

Old Estacio Padilla, on the other hand, took it quite seriously indeed. As a child, he himself had been carried off by marauding Indians, though they had been Comanche. Nonetheless, the Apache and Comanche were of a kind and none could say which might be worse. Estacio Padilla now in his sixties, was still a fine figure of a man, and when horseback, the equal of many men years younger.

Miss Fossie was mostly unconcerned regarding the matter as she had complete confidence in Estacio, as had her father before her. Estacio, in fact, pretty much ran the ranch and she had not been disappointed. There was no reason to believe that he could not handle the situation. She knew that few men understood Indians in general and the Comanche-Apache in particular as did her foreman. It was this confidence that caused her to turn down the offer of Frank Teal to take her with him back to town, this, even though Estacio himself encouraged her to avail herself of the opportunity. "No, I guess I'd best not," she said, flouncing up the steps to the house; causing Frank Teal to curse under his breath and spit tobacco juice into the red dust of the yard. Frank had long had an eye for Ella May and on the long trip out from town had been building, in his mind, quite a scenario involving the two of them.

...

That night, as Frank Teal lie broken and dying amid the wreckage of his empty freight-wagon, he came to a fuller appreciation of Ella May's remarkable intuition. In the dark, he had not seen the railroad tie Johnny Hat and his bunch had wrestled onto the narrow roadbed across

Arroyo Seco. It had taken a lot of effort to get that tie worked loose from the rip-rap of the culvert and up onto the road; but it had been worth it.

Frank's last thoughts were of Ella May flouncing up the steps of the Fossie house, holding her skirts just above her trim ankles.

Johnny Hat thought it fortuitous that the wreck alone had killed Frank Teal. There would be no real evidence to connect his death to the missing Indians. He knew enough about white men to understand the real danger lie not in the pursuing government agents, but in the local citizens should their ire be aroused. The Indians replaced the railroad tie and brushed out their tracks – although the two Navajos thought it an unnecessary trouble. The Apaches, however, having more experience in this sort of thing, made a point of it; at the same time allowing the team of horses to drift a good way up the rocky draw before apprehending them. There, they stripped them of their harness, which they buried, making it appear that the horses had wandered off on their own. Johnny Hat took the lesser damaged of the two geldings and gave the other to Big Nose, the more formidable of the three Jicarilla. Neither of the two saw fit to share their mounts and so the remainder of the band with some muted grumbling set out behind them on foot.

Their total take from the wrecked wagon, other than the horses, was Frank's nearly new lever-action rifle in 45-70 Government, a handful of cartridges, and a small case of salt pork. The Fossie ranch cook had turned the salt pork back, declaring it a little overly ripe. The Indians, however, looked upon the salt pork as a particular windfall. They had become used to bad Government pork down on the Bosque and had acquired a taste for it.

It was nearly daylight when the two lead Apaches heard the crowing of Ella May's Leghorn rooster and halted their horses on a small rise just south of the ranch. As they waited for the remainder of the band to straggle up, Big Nose mentioned the possibility of obtaining additional mounts. He also thought it would be good to have a few more rifles of the type now carried by Johnny Hat. Johnny Hat, already in possession of a horse and rifle, was not so sure it was worth the risk.

Big Nose put it as delicately as possible, given the other's reputation. "My friend, I appreciate the manner in which you divided these horses back there," he said, jerking a thumb back over his shoulder, "...even though this one is lame in the front-end and will doubtlessly have to be put to rest soon." He cleared his throat politely and went on, "There is, however, still the matter of the gun, which I ...if you'll remember... found lying under the white man and brought to show you as a matter of courtesy."

Johnny Hat pursed his lips, looking thoughtfully to the east where a fine line of gray was pushing back the night. For a moment Big Nose thought the Mescalero had not heard this last part about the gun and was preparing to reiterate, when Johnny Hat turned to him and Big Nose could see the glittering slits of his eyes in the darkness. "You did not mean for me to have it then..." Johnny Hat whispered, "...You would like it back..." his voice was velvet and did not carry to the others who were moving up from behind.

Big Nose shifted uncomfortably on his lame horse, "Well no ...of course... I mean there are plenty more where that came from." Big Nose nervously eyed the approaching dawn, "It's just that we may not have the opportunity further on..."

Johnny Hat said nothing as he toyed with the rifle's hammer in the darkness, clicking it back and forth in such a manner as to make Big Nose wish he had waited a while to bring up the subject. Finally Johnny Hat turned to the others who had silently moved up behind them. "My friend Big Nose thinks we could use some more horses ...and perhaps a few more rifles. He thinks it would be worth the risk, though we are only one gun and you others might be hard pressed to escape with your lives should we be discovered." He said this in a detached manner as though discussing the probability of the upcoming dawn. The two Navajos immediately declared their ability to walk to the Indian Territory given a couple of hours rest and a good bait of salt pork. The other two Jicarilla looked cautiously at Big Nose, whom they considered their leader only by default, knowing full well that bigger is not smarter.

Broken Hand, the remaining Mescalero, and Johnny Hat's uncle, moved to the front of the group. He was especially dark even for a Mescalero and wizened beyond his forty-five years. It was said he had killed several white men in his youth and Mexicans too numerous to mention. He also had a special skill with horses and was known to be the equal of any Comanche when it came to stealing them. "Brothers," he said, looking only at the Apaches, "...like these two Diné, I too feel certain I could walk to the Territory and that might be the safer plan. But I must warn you that it is still a long way off and we are likely to run into trouble yet. With horses we might be better able to elude those troubles," here he paused for effect, "...and we would be somebody when we arrive. I dislike the thoughts of coming into a new country on foot like a beggar ...or sheepherder." Once again he indicated the two Navajos, who looked away pretending not to understand. "My nephew here has spoken wisely of the danger to those of us without horses or weapons. You must know by now that always he has our best interest at heart." The Navajos looked suspiciously at Johnny Hat. "That is why I now take it upon myself to offer to go down to that ranch and look into this horse situation." This was a long speech for a man who, normally, didn't talk a great deal. Everyone now looked at Johnny Hat to see how he would take this talk from Broken Hand. He sat his horse quietly for a moment as though deep in thought. Finally he spoke. "Well, I see that it is in your heads to have those horses and if that is the way of it, I will do what I can to help, but I have a bad feeling about it." And with this he motioned Broken Hand off the rise toward the ranch. He then turned to Big Nose, "The guns will be in the big house. As soon as Broken Hand has the horses moving there will be dogs barking and then men shooting. As the vaqueros chase after Broken Hand there should be plenty of time for you to find those guns and maybe some food. Take these two with you." he said pointing at the other two Jicarilla. "And you," he said to the Navajos, "...take Big Nose's horse and circle to the west of the ranch where you will wait for these others to bring what they find."

"Where will you be?" Big Nose asked without thinking.

Johnny Hat gave him a sharp look, turned his horse without answering, and faded into the dark.

...

Estacio Padilla followed Ella May into the house as Frank Teal clucked sadly to his team and faced the long road back to town. The two of them watched from the parlor window as the wagon disappeared in a haze of dust. "That one thinks he would make a good husband and rancher." Estacio smiled.

"That one," Ella May said, shaking her dark curls "is as full of crap as a Christmas turkey."

Estacio rolled his eyes. He disliked rough talk in a woman and felt somehow responsible for Ella May being a little lax in that regard. After her mother died, Ella May had depended on Estacio for most of her upbringing – her own father not being of a suitable nature for it. Now Ella May looked more and more to Estacio, not that she would have admitted it of course.

She went to the kitchen and came back with the blue granite coffee pot and two porcelain cups. As she and Estacio sat at the parlor table looking out the bay window, she broached the subject that was on both their minds. "Do you think they will come?"

"We are directly in their path and the only water for ten miles. They will pass by here... if they haven't already." this, hoping Ella May might think it a possibility. He took a slow drink of his coffee, "Couldn't come at a worse time either, with only me and Cookie and Delbert left ...and Delbert with a broken arm." He squinted out the window to the East and the beginning of the Llano. He knew that somewhere out there was the rest of the crew just starting the spring gather. They would not be back for a while. It would be a full day's ride to the cow-camp at Stinking Wells, and another one back, leaving no one, to speak of, at the ranch. He wished now he had not sent both dogs on the gather, but who could have known? Finally he decided it would be best for her to be prepared. "That one they call Johnny Hat." he said touching his hat-brim, "...Es un hombre muy malo."

"You know him?"

"I know **of** him," his eyes went flat, "He's a breed. His father was a Commanchero, half-Mexican, half-white. Though, he claims to hate them both like the devil. By himself, he has more guts than a government mule ...and if it's true Big Nose is with him ...Ayeee, Dios mio."

"Do you think they've gone by us already?"

"No," he admitted, "If they had gone by us we would be missing something. They have not come this far ...which means they have no horses." his voice became hard, "Which means they will want ours." He sat his cup down carefully. "They will be here ...by and by."

...

Ella May sat by the open window of her upstairs bedroom looking out over the front yard. She could just see the corner of the barn and corrals in the dim light of a little half moon. Clouds occasionally scudded across the moon, plunging the ranch yard into total darkness. The soft smell of the flowering mesquite was in the breeze that toyed with the lace curtains. Somewhere a bitch coyote gave her little yip ...yip, the signal to her mate that she was leaving the pups for the evening hunt. That is, if it were a Coyote at all. She wondered if Estacio, rolled in his blankets near the front door, could hear it ...could tell if it were a coyote or Apache. She knew Estacio's hearing was not what it once was, still she felt better for him being there. Her fingertips traced the engraving on the English double she held in her lap. Her father would have been pleased with the choice. He never thought her much of a rifle shot. She had six loads of double-ought buck-shot lined up on the window sill. You could take a man off a horse at fifty yards with such a load Estacio said, of course the chances were, you would take out the horse too – maybe her own horse – but that couldn't be helped.

Cookie was covering the rear of the house from the bunkhouse door. Delbert was in the haymow over the barn where he had a clear view of the corrals and the near side of the house. They were ready. If those bucks came tonight, Ella May thought, they would be in some serious trouble. This was her ranch now. Her Father had slick-ered the Mexicans out of it, and fought the Comanche for it, and worked himself to death on it. It would take more than this "Johnny in a Hat" to steal what was hers.

. . .

The two Navajos were crouched in a little sand wash just west of the ranch buildings, waiting for something to happen. They talked softly in their own tongue. They were tired of the Apaches and their hard ways, tired of listening to the harsh guttural boasting of Big Nose and the other two Jicarilla ...even worse were the baleful stares of the two Mescalero. The more outspoken of the two said he didn't think Johnny Hat was so tough ...but he whispered when he said it.

The second one nodded a cautious agreement. He too thought the Apaches a little overrated. "These Apaches are not our kind of people." he said, "I have been think-ing that maybe it was not so good an idea, this running for the Territory. Oh, it's fine for them. Their friends will fix a place for them. But we know no one there and I can see now that these Apaches do not intend to help us."

"Those were my thoughts also," the other admitted picking up a handful of sand and letting it run through his fingers, "In the canyons it is time to plant corn and hold the dances." In a small voice he sang a few words of the corn planting song, shaking his head sadly, "My heart is no longer in this thing. I say we return to our own country. In the canyon-lands we still have family to hide us. Perhaps the government will forget about us and we can quit this hard life." Their eyes met in the graying dawn. Silently, as one, they rose and mounted double on the lame horse, pointing his nose to the west ...taking with them, the last of the salt pork.

...

Broken Hand silently gnashed his teeth as he examined the corral from the shadows of the barn. There were only three horses. They would still be two horses short. Those Navajos would just be out of luck he smiled.

He had taken particular pains to arrive downwind in case of dogs, but so far none were apparent. He faintly heard Big Nose and his Jicarilla coming down the hill and knew they would be waiting for him to start something. Other than the horses dozing at the feed rack there were no signs of life ...in it-self a bad sign. A rosy pink glow was on the eastern horizon. There should have been a cook or woman stirring. This was too easy to his way of thinking. He knew now what Johnny Hat had meant by 'a bad feeling'. He slipped along the corral in the shadows until he reached the pole-gate, which he unlatched and left ajar. Keeping the feed rack between him and the horses, he clucked softly so they would know someone was there, and not bolt when he appeared.

For just an instant something seemed to catch his eye at the opening to the haymow over the barn, a flicker, a bat maybe. He studied the opening carefully but could see nothing.

The horses were watching him intently now though they showed no sign of fear. Good! They were gentle saddle stock, used to being handled in the dark. He pulled a thin leather thong from around his waist and moved confidently to the side of a big bay gelding, which reached out its nose, snuffing at his hand. Carefully, he slipped one arm around the horse's neck and with the other hand secured a loop to the gelding's lower jaw. He had watched long enough to know this gelding was the ringleader. That would make things a lot easier. He would ride out at a gallop and the other two would follow. That's the way it was with horses, he smiled ...and with Indians too. He was thinking of Big Nose and his two Jicarilla waiting now in the brush beyond the front yard of the house.

As he flung himself onto the big gelding's back and jump-started him for the gate there was a picture in his mind of how good he would look riding into the Territory on this horse.

The ball from Delbert's 38-40 caught Broken Hand just behind the left ear and Broken Hand was to ride that bay gelding into eternity.

...

Johnny Hat sat his horse, nearly hidden among the yuccas, on a little ridge north of the ranch. He thought this would be a good place to cover Broken Hand's retreat and possibly help with the new horses. His old uncle had apparently not lost his touch, as not even a dog had barked so far. Hunger was starting to gnaw at his belly and he hoped Big Nose might come back with enough food to last them to the Territory. Those two Navajos were eating them out of house and home ...so to speak. He would be glad when they were through this country and across the Llano. That Llano was the worst possible kind of country for an Apache ...flat, barren ...no place to hide. He would feel better in Oklahoma where he was told there would be some hills and cover. He felt agitated and anxious somehow. It must be that little bit of white blood in him, he thought, that kept him always so stirred up inside.

He hoped Big Nose would not feel the need to kill anyone down there. Not that it would bother him personally, but he hated the thought of that kind of trouble following them to Oklahoma Territory, where it might not be appreciated. In any case he would be glad to be rid of Big Nose and his Jicarilla once they were among the Comanche. Big Nose was not smart enough to stay out of trouble very long.

...

At that moment Big Nose and his men lie hidden in the thick mesquite beyond the ranch yard where they could see the corrals and the front of the house. They were waiting only for Broken Hand and the horse herd to provide a little cover. They were surprised there was no dog. These white men always kept a dog. They shook their heads smiling at one another; it would be just like the white's to have the dog inside. Big Nose grinned as his hand found his knife. He would show these white people a thing or two about dogs.

It was getting light enough now to make out the open window over the front porch. Big Nose could see the lace curtains moving in the breeze and nudged his companions, pointing it out. Then, smiling to himself, he slipped away in the murky dawn. The remaining two Jicarilla looked at one another in consternation. This had not been the plan! What of Broken Hand and the horses? The diversion! This changing of plans at the last minute ...no good could come of it.

...

Old Estacio was awake now, though he had dozed off a couple of times during the night, lying there on the floor. He had not meant to and chided himself as he peered out the crack of the open door. He knew from his years with the Comanche that the old adage about Indians not attacking at night was bullshit. These were renegades ...cholos, who might do God knew what. There was a small cold thing in the pit of his stomach as he thought about what Apaches were capable of. He would shoot El-la May himself before letting them.... A Coyote yelped down by the spring and was answered by a long thin wail above the ranch. Each morning since the dogs left, the pair had finished their nightly hunt with a drink at the spring. The female would then return to the pups while the male came to the barn to check on the chickens, hoping against hope that one, in a fit of greed, might fly down a little early. This morning, however, something had come between the two coyotes. Something whose smell they didn't like. Estacio thought he knew what it was.

As the blast of Delbert's 38-40 bounced back and forth between the barn and house, Ella May jerked bolt upright in her rocker – coming face to face with her first Apache. Big Nose, standing tiptoe on the porch roof was trying to hold on with one hand while reaching for the sleeping girl's shotgun. For him, Delbert's shooting had come at the worst possible time. Ella May's shotgun had been pointing a little below the windowsill and her reflex reaction was to pull both triggers. This, of course, eliminated the windowsill and the Apache all in one motion.

At the first sound of gunfire from the barn, the two Jicarilla left in hiding sprung from the mesquite and were nearly half way to the house when they saw Big Nose doing a back-flip, off the porch roof, amid a shower of shingles and siding. They saw at once that Big Nose was no longer a determining factor in their lives. "This is what comes of changing plans!" one shouted, as they ran back to the mesquite in a hail of bullets. In the poor light of dawn Estacio's old eyes were not taking good aim and firepower alone could not make up for it.

Years later when the two Jicarilla were themselves old men, they would occasionally recall for one another how Big Nose looked doing a back-flip off the porch ...and would laugh uproariously... far beyond the actual humor in the thing.

The trickle of light in the East became a stream, and then a torrent, finally inundating the ranch in a brilliant flood. Johnny Hat, still sitting his horse on the little ridge, could plainly see his uncle, Broken Hand; obviously dead, lying in the center of the corral with the three horses still milling about. What was left of Big Nose was sprawled in the front yard like a broken Kachina doll. He watched closely as an old man and a white woman with dark curly hair came out to inspect their work. The woman nudged Big Nose with the toe of her shoe as she held her gun at the ready ...but there was no fight left in Big Nose.

Slowly, Johnny Hat turned toward the sunrise and the vastness of the Llano. The air was crisp and clean with the fresh new smell of the dawn and he could see many miles across the silent sweep of the grasslands. Somewhere there was the sweet warble of a Meadowlark but no living creature stirred that he could see. The Comanche were gone now ...and the buffalo, leaving only a great empty space ...which in the end, would be filled up with these white people.

Cliff Dwellers

Shy, they hover in the shadows
along the broken ledges
still as idols in the twilight
as they contemplate the scene

from their dwellings in the darkness
I almost feel them at the edges
of the hollow doors and windows
As I ford their little stream

as sunset flings it's arrows
in a final parting volley
it illuminates the kivas
to rekindle ancient soul

and canyon walls re-echo
with the mystery of their folly
once again they come to season
by the magic of its glow.

slowly darkness cloaks the Mesa
and their scurry's all around me
as my campfire warms the flavor
of the pinyon scented air

and softly through the somber
I sense them reaching, almost touch me
as they shimmer on the fringes
in little shows of ghostly dare

from the broken pots around me
I cull a shard of subtle lining
and an instant silvery laughter
seems to float upon the breeze

while I peer into the darkness
hoping for some secret signing
of the potter as she hides there
in the scatter of the trees

gone, these thousand years now
in their natural and good order
still they roam the hidden reaches
...archaic margins of my mind

 and they call me, seem to know me
from an age beyond some border
where the eons gather stardust
from a people lost in time.

Dart Smith

Buzzards circle above the old man's shack like flies over a privy. There's something bad down there and they know it. If they could see inside the cabin, they wouldn't like it. The old man isn't dead yet – it's just a matter of time before he is of course – but not quite yet.

"That's how it goes," the old man sings softly to himself, "…first your money, then your clothes." He thinks it has been about three days since he broke his leg but has drifted in and out of consciousness so often it has skewed his mental clock, leaving him dangling in the ether somewhere. It had been a hard pull back up to the shack, crawling along on his belly like a reptile.

There is water in the bucket beside the stove and a pan of dried up cornbread in the oven; he hums in a small cracked voice between bites and swallows of tepid water. He hesitates to crawl back to the open door but knows that could be his last chance. Anyone passing through that country will have to come within hailing distance of the shack, the canyon narrows that much. Anyone will do, he thinks, a cowboy or drifter, lord even a Mexican or Indian might work.

A horse, still saddled, loafs in the shade by the corral, switching flies and keeping an eye on the buzzards. There's plenty of feed and it won't leave, though it has tried to roll the saddle off a few times.

"Serves ya right!" the old man croaks when finally he reaches the open door, but it comes out just a rusty squeak, with no real malice behind it. Damned fresh colt that he was – no, it had been his own fault alright, he should have known better, did, in fact, know better. It's just that it was such an easy shot, right by the cabin and all, and who knows what that buck might have done should he have dismounted first. Well the buck is dead, for what little good it will do anyone now. It just went to prove the old adage: 'You can shoot off any horse …once.' That's what the buzzards are in the neighborhood for, that, and some buzzardly premonition that all is not well in the shack. The leg no longer hurts, to speak of, despite the yellowed shards of bone poking out. The blood, matted up around the wool pants and bones, forms a blackened poultice. Even so, the leg is terribly swollen and has the odor of death about it. It will have to come off no matter what, but he doesn't hold much hope even for that unhappy eventuality.

He's tired now and it seems hardly worth the effort to stay awake, keep watch. He had always hoped he would go out quick and quiet when his time came, "not waller around in my own do'ins for three days."

The sun is beginning to edge down behind the canyon rim leaving a soft amber glow in the creek bottom. The old man hates to see it go. He has an idea morning might be a long time coming – never – is the word that comes to his mind. He wishes he had gotten up early more often …to see the sun rise. As the last light seeps out of the canyon, he manages to prop himself up against the doorpost. He reaches for the old shotgun, lays it beside him, and drawing a blanket over his legs, he waits. He figures to go out "vertical."

.....

Tyrone Dartwilder Smith's horse was on his last legs, a full night and day, mostly at a trot, had taken it all out of him. A good horse, but not the horse he had wanted. The horse he had wanted belonged to a little whore named Dolly May Sissom. It had been tied too close to the saloon door to have any real hope of success. He had settled instead on this big black gelding, nearly as black as himself he thinks with some satisfaction – good night horse for his line of work. It had been tied in the alley behind the saloon and belonged to a nearly bald-headed solicitor, recently from back east, and still cautious of his reputation.

It wouldn't have mattered to "Dart" Smith that he had stolen the horse of the only defense attorney within two hundred miles. Defense attorneys would have little to do with it should he happen to be caught. And being caught is the last thing on his mind this early June night of 1902 in New Mexico territory.

What is on his mind, is a coffee-colored girl in Denver, several hundred miles to the north – that, and the three hundred and fifty-two dollars she had talked him into leaving with her. That three hundred and fifty two dollars is the most money he has ever come by and as badly as he wants it back, he knows there are two sheep men out of Wyoming who want it back just as badly. They aren't likely to forget about it ...or let the law forget about it either. Six months, however, should be as good as it is going to get. He is tired of sleeping out and he is tired of eating rabbits – he has eaten a God's plenty of them and they are starting to lay a little heavy on his soul.

It has been a long hard circle to the west, then north, with the hope of slipping into Colorado through the back door. That might have been possible too, if it hadn't been for the necessity of snatching up this new horse. This horse will throw a whole new slant on the odds. There is nothing for it now, however, and Dart smith urges the failing mount on. He knows horses and anticipates doing some serious walking before morning. He is not a big man, nor particularly strong, but he is unusually determined in what he does, and has an uncommon amount of what people like to refer to as gumption. There is an aura about him that men can sense – not danger exactly - it's more of an extract of that quality, which in some strong way makes men aware they are dealing with the real article. "Don't mess with Dart Smith!" They tell one another, "He won't tolerate it!"

The moon comes up loud and brassy. He has never seen such moons as they have in this country. They just seem to jump up on the horizon. They can jangle a man right out of his blankets on a soft summer night. He calculates he could shoot a man off a horse at two hundred yards in such light; allowing he had a gun that could shoot two hundred yards, which he doesn't. What he has is a wore-out .38-40 Winchester, anything past a hundred yards and he might as well be throwing rocks into a bucket. He intends to get himself something with a little more authority when he gets his hands on that money.

It is past midnight when the horse gives out completely, first slowing to a stumbling walk, then, going down in the front end. Dart Smith steps off with a sigh as the horse crumples. It had been a good horse ...for an eastern horse ...some sort of Saddle-bred or Tennessee walker maybe. He reaches down and jerks loose the latigo, releasing the cinch. He hates to leave that saddle – it's a custom job by a well-known Missouri maker and fits him to a T. He hefts it a couple of times with the idea in mind of taking it along, but that wouldn't make sense. His coat, rifle and canteen will be plenty before this night is over.

He is well off the main trail, in the cedars, and was riding up a gravel wash when the horse went down. It is a simple matter now to conceal it with brush and rock. Dart Smith is well versed in the manner of staying ahead of the law and he prides himself on leaving no stone unturned in the process, "Ain't gonna be no tattle-tale buzzards," he grunts, as he lays a final sandstone slab. "Mother Smith never raised so foolish a child."

...

It is just breaking daylight when the old man's horse whinnies down the canyon. Dart Smith knows he is coming up on something, a ranch maybe, or a camp. ...Something. He has cut directly cross-country taking advantage of the moonlight to negotiate a series of canyons and cedar draws. He guesses, all in all, he has put nearly a hundred miles between him and the town – a long way in that country. He slips into the brush along the creek and eases up on the shack with his rifle cocked. He has six cartridges left, all of them in the magazine. He wonders what it will work out to, in terms of bullets per person, should it come to that.

...

The old man is happy – heaven is just as he thought it might be. He floats on woolly white clouds across verdant meadows bejeweled with sparkling blue pools. The glow of divine providence is on his face and the cool nectar of the gods, poured by an angel, soothes his parched throat. His eyelids flutter open toward the warmth of its benevolence.

"...A nigger angel?" He asks in a small voice, trying to focus on Dart Smith. The angel is eating a piece of cornbread as he holds the cup to the old man's lips. "I didn't expect no nigger angels," the old man murmurs in disbelief. "And I was hoping for something more than cornbread too. Oh, it's alright, I guess," he adds not wanting to appear ungrateful. "It's just that I was thinking more along the lines of ...oh, I don't know, maybe some rhubarb pie."

The angel is licking his fingers, smiling and shaking his head. "No, you ol' bastard it's cornbread for everbody up here, white and black alike." He chuckles, wiping his hands on his vest.

The old man opens one eye wider, "That's not much of a way for an angel to talk. I must be way down on the list to deserve no better than this."

"I expect that's about right," Dart Smith chuckles again. "You got any money around here old man?"

"Well ...hell," The old man sighs, peering hard now at Dart Smith, "...you ain't no angel, and this ain't heaven." He's right back in his own shack, being robbed. "I knowed there weren't no nigger angels." He sighs.

Dart Smith is rummaging around in some baking powder tins on the shelf behind the stove. "An old cracker like you must have a few dollars around here somewhere. Ain't that right old man? ...and we know you ain't gonna be need'n it."

The old man's head is swimming and his bleary eyes can barely follow Dart Smith as he pokes and digs around in the meager furnishings. He isn't afraid or even particularly upset. The boy's right – he ain't going to be needing it. Still, "You don't know anything about cuttin' off legs do you boy?"

Dart Smith stops momentarily to stare at the old man, snorting, "Cuttin' off legs? ...Cuttin' off LEGS! You must still be dreamin' old man. If I did know something about cuttin' off legs, which I don't, I'd be wasting both our time. Uh-uh," he says looking at the old man's leg, "...that trains done gone by."

The old man's eyes narrow in the dim light of the shack – a tear rolls down his cheek, "Well, I guess she'll never get it then," ...as though to himself, "I reckon she'll just have to make out the best she can ...without that money I been saving for her dowry." His voice breaks, "the poor fat little thing, she'll likely never get a husband now."

Dart Smith was reaching for the rifle hanging over the bed on pegs; it is partially obscured by old coats and hats. "Hot damn!" he exclaims, "a Yellow Boy!" He pulls down the lever-action Henry with its solid brass receiver. "Happy day!" he exclaims again, "It's a 44-40 Government, just what I always wanted." He brings the rifle to his shoulder and sights down the long octagonal barrel, "ain't hardly been used by the look of it," he declares. Two hundred yards wouldn't be out of the question with a rifle like this. He levers it open a crack, seeing that it is indeed loaded. "You got any more cartridges for this?" He asks, turning to the old man.

He is looking directly into the twin holes of a hammers-back, sawed off, 12 gauge shot gun.

"I figured to signal with this if anyone come riding by ...and sure enough, someone has," the old man cackles weakly.

Dart Smith has the Henry pointed toward the old man but will have to pull back the hammer if anything is to come of it.

"If you even twitch; I'm gonna take out that whole wall," the old man assures him, painfully shifting his good knee up under the shotgun barrels. "I was saying... now, there's no way my daughter will ever get her...."

"I heard you the first time." Dart Smith shakes his head, "Damned old liar. You're not talking to some hillbilly fool here. Dart Smith has been down the road and back and damned if I'll fall for such as that!" Even if he can take the old man, he knows it's likely the shotgun will go off in the process ...and he's right about it taking out the whole wall.

"Well Sir! Looks like what we got here is a Mex'can stand-off ...except for one thing," the old man grimaces.

"And what might that be?" Dart smith asks, surreptitiously easing his thumb over the hammer.

The old man readjusts his position with a pained expression, "Well, you see, I've already gotten used to the idea of dying ...and you ain't. It don't hardly bother me none now. Oh, I'd prefer not to, but when you get my age, a little time, one way or the other ain't all that important." The old man paused, and spat weakly out the door. "I ain't got no daughter ...but the part about the money's true, there's a lard pail full of it buried just up the canyon a piece ...course I ain't going to tell you where, and you'd play hell finding it on your own." The old man pauses, his breathing ragged, "But if you was to take this leg off ...and I did accidentally live through it, that money would be all yours, not to mention the Henry, and the saddle horse outside. I'd sign 'em over to you right now." The old man is having trouble holding his head up straight.

"Ha! The gun and horse are already mine, and I still don't think you got any money worth the trouble." Dart Smith's thumb is covering the hammer now and he is playing for time, he can see the old man is fading.

"Well, look at it this way," the old man says, almost in a whisper, "If I got well and there weren't no money you could still kill me. You don't think I'd put myself through a leg cuttin' just to get shot ...do you?

Dart Smith's thumb wavered over the hammer, "...and what if I go to all this trouble and you die anyway?"

"Them's the breaks," the old man cackles feebly, "You'd still have a horse and gun and papers to go with 'em. ...I can't see you have much to lose except'n a little time ...and maybe that cornbread you just ate." He gave another gravelly laugh that trailed off into a hacking cough. He is having difficulty keeping the black man in focus.

Dart Smith is in a quandary – he has to admit, it wouldn't make sense for the old man to offer such a deal without something to back it up. And he does know how to use a meat saw alright. He helped out around the field hospital when he was soldiering – enough to know this is a long shot at best. But he also knows he wouldn't have to wait around very long afterward for the results. "How much money we talk'n about old man?" The old man can't hear him very well now and Dart Smith has to repeat the question, "I Say! How much you reckon it is?"

The old man is uncertain, "I figure it to be over five hundred dollars, give or take a little." He knows it isn't near that much, but he expects five hundred dollars will sound good to Dart Smith. He is starting to wish Dart Smith would just go ahead and shoot him. His lips are starting to go numb and he wipes his mouth with the back of his hand. He can feel it all slipping away, one way or the other, he is making his final deal.

....

"Damned ol' reprobate," Dart Smith mutters to himself as he gathers up wood under the wash boiler in the front-yard. The thought of cutting off the leg is causing the corn bread in his stomach to float a little, "There ain't no way he's gonna make it..." he says under his breath, ...still, five hundred dollars is a pile of money, and he has spent most of his life pursuing long shots far less lucrative. He does, certainly, intend to shoot the old man the instant he should find there is no money ...It would only be right ...and it was the deal.

He decides to do the cuttin' right there on the front porch, where the light is good, and the cabin won't be ruined. He looks forward to sleeping under a roof for a change. He has found a piece of fairly clean canvas and puts it under the unconscious old man and then cuts off his trouser leg, working around the congealed mass of the wound. He wishes he could remember more about how the army doctors had worked. He had once seen them take off a man's arm that had been smashed in a wagon wreck ...not a pretty sight, but at least they'd had something fresh to work with ...this would be another matter entirely.

There is a jug of white liquor under the bed and it is all he can do to hold himself to two drinks. He sets the jug beside the old man and makes a tourniquet from his belt, tightening it just below the old man's hip. If he is going to do it he might as well do it right, taking too little is as bad as not doing it at all – one of the army doctors had said that – it had, for some reason, stuck in his mind. A pail of boiled water, flour sacks, and the meat saw is at hand, as is a scuttle of hot coals with a stove poker in it. There is a fine bone-handled butcher knife, nearly new, and exceedingly sharp, which he holds over the coals until the blade begins to turn blue.

He works quickly, the morning sun only now falling on the front porch. The leg is as clean as it will get, and has been wiped down with a rag soaked in liquor. Occasionally he has to raise his nose to the breeze coming up the canyon to get by the stench. He positions two pieces of stove-wood, one under the old man's hip and the other under the knee. The old man has neither moved nor made a sound and it is only with close inspection that Dart Smith can tell that he still lives. "Lordy... Lordy... Lordy... he says to himself.

He intends to make one sweeping cut from underneath, to the outside, then around to the top – leaving the inside of the leg with its pulsing artery till the last possible instant, when he will snatch up the poker and seal it. There is a small piece of wood, wrapped in cloth, under the tourniquet, pressing directly on the vessel, but he knows it won't be enough. The actual sawing will be the least of it. He has taken the precaution of tying the old man's hands behind his head, to a heavy log bench, and his good leg to the porch railing. He will sit on him if he has to – it isn't just the money now – he wants to do this thing right.

The old man does not dream and comes directly from the depths of a black well to an immediate state of awareness. There is a soft breeze wafting through the tiny window at the foot of the bed, bringing with it the distant sound of a spiritual sung in a low clear voice. The warmth of the sun, shimmering through the willow leaves outside the window, causes the old man to sigh. He doesn't bother to look down at his leg; it is gone, or he wouldn't be here. Probably, it has been several days now. There doesn't seem to be near the pain he thought there would be. A pot of something on the stove is simmering one or two bubbles at time, it smells good, and has to do with rabbits if the old man is any judge.

The cabin is clean and there is a cup of fresh water by the bed. A wave of contentment washes over the old man, and he smiles as he looks up to see the Henry still hanging over the bed. He wonders if the black man has found the saddle gun down by the corral, the one he dropped, when the horse threw him. He'd had that gun a long time and thought more of it than he did the Henry. As he looks around he sees that the black man has made a pallet on the floor near the head of the bed that he might be close by in the night. A great sadness falls over the old man now, as he lies staring at the ceiling. He has known a good many bad men in his time, most folks don't know what a really bad man is, but he had been one himself and knows one when he sees him. It takes everything he has to reach up and lift down the Henry. It appears to be freshly cleaned and oiled. He levers in one of the big brass cartridges with its 200 grain, round nose bullet, watching it disappear into the breach with a soft click. Lifting himself on one elbow, he calls through the little window, "Boy! ...Come see how good the old man is!" This Dart Smith is the kind of man who would think a deal is a deal.

The Rooster fighter

Toot got out of bed fairly early for a man who had been drunk for three days. He carried his face in his two hands, stepping carefully, like an old woman with a basket of eggs. He's had plenty of hangovers, but this one is a real noodle-thumper. Gravitating instinctively toward the kitchen, he stands a moment in his stocking feet and long underwear, peering blearily out the window over the sink. Something is gnawing away at the back of his mind. It will come to him he knows and he waits for it as one waits for a bus in a bad part of town.

Being one of those rare men who can eat, regardless of circumstance, he now sets about preparing a staggering meal, handling the iron skillets like fine china, lest the smallest clink kill him outright. He has to set down at the table from time to time, putting his head between his legs. Toot takes pride in the fact that he has never puked from drink, nor passed out either, extraordinary feats when you consider the scope of his indulgence.

The bacon is beginning to sizzle and curl by the time the coffee is ready, and he has a large pile of sliced potatoes ready to slide into the hot fat. He hopes he's wrong about Norma Jean Petty, but he seldom forgets anything he's done when drinking and the chances of it not having happened are slim indeed.

He shudders, as a wave of nausea sweeps him back into the chair, cursing himself, swearing this is the end of it, just as he always does. He walks to the back-bedroom door and calls as softly as possible "Johnny Bob! You'd best get your butt out here if you want to eat! I ain't cleaning up two messes this morning." He goes back to his chair with his fingertips holding his temples together. "I don't believe I can clean up two messes this morning." He tells the floor in a small voice.

"Johnny! Was Norma Jean over here this morning about daylight?" He calls again, maintaining a steady pressure with his fingers to avoid an aneurysm.

Johnny Bob came through the door zipping up his Levis and chuckling, "Yes sir, she was ...and she was hotter'n a two peckered billy-goat too!"

"You watch your mouth – I don't want to hear that kind of trash out of you." Toot wasn't fooling either.

His son rubbed the sleep out of his eyes. "I don't believe I ever saw her that mad before," he chortled, looking out the window. "I'll swear I don't know what that woman sees in you, daddy."

Toot groaned and rose to the stove. The bacon was draining, now, on a brown paper sack and the potatoes were nearly perfect. "...Because... I'm a hell of a cook – that's what – now how many eggs you want while I'm up here?"

"Two or three I guess."

Johnny Bob liked his eggs over-easy, but knew there was no use in asking - Toot wouldn't be up to anything fancy. "Just go ahead and scramble 'em," he whispers as he sees Toot stirring them together with a fork. "How much did you lose yesterday, anyhow? Dib Carter said you were throwing money around like we was printing it right here at home."

Toot winced, "Oh, Lord," That's what that little rat had been worrying the back edge of his brain about. He clutched the sink, "Nearly twelve hundred dollars..." there wasn't any need to lie about it, "And the car."

Johnny Bob sucked in his breath. "The **car**! Damn it! You lost the car?" The boy was beside himself. "That was going to be my car!"

"Yes, well, it's going to be Harv Maxwell's car now... and I don't want to hear any more about it." Toot rubbed his chin stubble thoughtfully "...course, he ain't got the title to it yet." He brightened considerably, "I might be able to work something out ...you never can tell. Maybe... I could call the sheriff and report it stolen." He squinted narrowly out the window, "that way we could maybe collect on the insurance or somethin" his voice trailed off hopelessly, "…uh ...no …that insurance ran out."

Johnny Bob sat down heavily in the other chair, shaking his head slowly in disbelief. This was much worse than he thought. It wasn't uncommon for Toot to lose a little money right along, fighting roosters, but this thing with the car was another matter entirely.

Father and son now both sat with their heads in their hands, the food growing cold on the table. "I knew I should have come with you Saturday," the boy sighed, though he knew it wouldn't have done any good. Toot had started drinking Friday and by fight time Saturday he wouldn't have paid him any more attention than a piss-ant. That's just the way he was when he was drinking. "What happened?" he asked, without any real interest.

"Well," Toot said, slowly raising his head, his eyes taking on a faraway look, "It beat anything ...I ever saw in my life." Toot commonly prefaced the most plausible occurrences with this statement and Johnny Bob closed his eyes and gritted his teeth. This was going to take a while.

"You remember that big old boy, comes from over around San Antonio? Fights them good little green legged red roosters... Delbert... something or other... it'll come to me. Well, anyhow he has a full show see, six nest brothers, like as peas in a pod. I helped him unload 'em myself. He's the feller that won the big five-cock derby last year! Said these were bred just like those others only a little better, if you know what I mean. Those birds were cackling and crowing and throwing straw out the slats like crazy. As you well know, I'm a pretty fair judge of a game-chicken myself and I could see these were dead-ready and sett'n on go. Delbert says to me... "Toot," he says. "You can bet a little money on these old roosters, I been raising 'em for thirty years and they don't owe me a dime."

Toot was getting a little color back now and looked over at the food with renewed interest. He began loading his plate as he talked. "I figured if I bet two hundred a' piece on them, I couldn't go wrong, even though I had to lay a hundred to eighty to get a bet." He was talking around a mouthful of eggs and potatoes now and Johnny Bob had to lean forward a little to understand. "Well sir, the first five of them fought like ducks, couldn't have whipped their own mama, and I had money down on ever' one. I just couldn't believe they would all lose." Toot was sweating now, only partly from the Red-Devil sauce he had sprinkled on his eggs. He was tapping the floor with one foot and developed a twitch at the corner of his mouth. "When they called his sixth fight I could see he was meeting Harley Struthers from Dallas, and Harley's five straight in the win column! Delbert comes over and says "Toot, Lord knows I'm sorry about all this... but this last rooster is the best 'un I believe I have ever owned... if ever a bird could win it's him. Now you do what you gotta do, but I'm gonna bet the ranch on him!" Toot reached and got another slice of bacon. "When they got in the pit the odds-makers were calling Delbert the dog and laying a hundred to sixty against him. You're grandmaw didn't raise no fools so I load up everything I have left... plus the car, on Harley's grey bird. I figure to get well in a hurry! Toot slowly chewed his bacon and stared, unseeing, past Johnny Bob, past the little rosebuds on the wallpaper.

Johnny Bob knew... but he had to ask anyway, "So what happened?"

"Oh, well, they met about head-high and Delbert's red rooster piled that Grey up in a corner like he'd been shot out of the air with a twelve gauge." He choked back a smile. "It nearly broke all the gamblers. Why Tuffy Smith had to hitch-hike back to Dallas!" Toot got a sad look on his face at the very thought of it.

"How'd you get back?"

"Hitch-hiked... but it ain't all that far, Dallas, on the other hand is a pretty good little jaunt. I hope Tuffy made it back alright."

Johnny Bob's sixteen years weighed heavily on him as he stared at his father. "I wouldn't be worrying about Tuffy Smith, if I were you! I'd be worrying about what we're going to be driving."

"Why, Hell, son, we still got the old pick-up truck!"

"The old pick-up truck?" The boy stared in disbelief, "I'd rather be walking along the inter-state carrying a Chevy hubcap than drive'n that old Ford."

"Well, you do as you think best, but I'm going to get the truck started and go into town ...find Norma Jean." Toot scratched his head. "Seems like I tried to explain everything to her this morning," He only vaguely re-membered Norma Jean being there. "Son, what was the last thing she said before she left?"

Johnny Bob looked at Toot a long time before an-swering. He raised his eyes to the ceiling and squinted at the light bulb. "She said... 'Tuffy Smith is a no good son-of-bitch ...and you one too!' Then... she kicked over the dog's water and ran out."

Toot looked genuinely surprised, "Why would she say that about Tuffy? She don't even know Tuffy!"

"Well, I would guess it was because you were trying to borrow her car so you could go find Tuffy and carry him back to Dallas."

Toot passed a hand nervously across his face, study-ing his plate with a blank look. "That Norma Jean's a case, ain't she, you never know what's gonna set her off." He sighed with a sad shake of his head and rose to face what he thought could be a rather unpromising day.

...

Toot wheeled the old Ford truck into the parking lot of the Hoppity Hop & Shop where Norma Jean Petty worked on Sundays after church. He sat there tapping the steering wheel in time to the ticking noise the engine made as it cooled. He could see Norma Jean behind the cash register, arms folded, staring icicles out the window at him. It was hard to believe they were going to be mar-ried next week ...that is... if they were, in fact, still going to be married next week. Getting out of the truck, he thought, fleetingly, that he might ought to leave the engine running, but instead, just smiled real big and waved. Thank God no one else was in the store. Norma Jean Petty was nobody's fool and Toot knew that every word would have to count.

My! My! Don't you look nice honey! How was church this morning... sweetie?"

Norma Jean shook her head, "Don't you Honey-Sweetie me... you no-count, loose bred, sorry excuse for a human being!

Toot moved back a step but kept smiling, "Now, darlin' there's no call to get all up..."

"Don't... Darlin'... me... Toot, You and me is through. You have played me for a fool for the last time and it'll be a cold day in hell when you and I have any more to talk about! Now get in that old wreck out there and get out of my life before I get the shot-gun after you!"

Toot's headache was back in full force and it was all he could do to keep his mouth shut as he backed out the door. He knew, now, that he had misjudged the time element involved. It would likely take several more days before she would be able to deal with this in a rational manner.

The old truck's engine clattered terribly as Toot pulled onto the hi-way, "I wish't I'd a thought to pick up a quart of oil while I was in there," he said to himself.

Toot's life was a shambles... son alienated... fiancée gone totally scattie-boo... he couldn't imagine where it would all end. "What I need is a drink," he said, pulling up in front of a beer-joint with a red neon sign that read; SNEAKY PETE'S BAR & Bar-B-Que.

The brakes were slow to catch and Toot instinctively jerked back on the steering wheel, which obligingly came off in his hands. The truck nudged on up to the cement porch with Toot yelling "Whoa!" at the top of his voice. He reached out and patted the dashboard, "Damned if we ain't hav'n a nice'un," he told the truck, reaching in his pocket for what was left of his money. "There's only about three dollars and twenty cents here," he estimated out loud, thinking guiltily of the quart of oil. "Looks like only one of us is gonna get lubricated." Toot carried the steering wheel inside with him and laid it up on the bar. Tubby Wilson was polishing a glass and smiled, "Toot, I don't believe there's any need in carrying that with you. Nobody's gonna steal that truck of yours."

The Johnson brothers down at the end of the bar laughed – way out of proportion to the joke – they didn't have good sense, Toot thought, and thus were easily amused.

He grinned "You never know. I hear there's some desperate characters hangs out in here."

Tubby chuckled, pouring a double Jack with water by it. "Heard what happened up at the fights... sounds like you had quite a day!" He set the drink on the bar, winking, "This one's on the house," which caused the Johnson brothers to frown. It had been a good while since Tubby had bought them a drink.

"I 'preciate that Tubby, but I do have enough left to buy a drink," Toot said.

"Well, I should say you should," Tubby laughed, winking again.

Tubby must have had a few himself Toot thought, swirling the liquor around in his glass before tossing it off in one smooth motion. He was surprised it didn't really taste all that good... even being free. He wiped his mouth, picked up the steering wheel and stepped down off the stool. It had been a long day and it wasn't over yet. "See you boys, I've got to get home before dark ...headlights don't work."

Tubby ambled over to the window to watch Toot pounding the steering wheel back on his truck. "That Toot, he's a caution ain't he..." he paused thoughtfully, "...the Lord loves a plunger though!"

...

Toot drove slowly up in the yard, letting the truck gear itself to a stop. It wasn't until he got out that he noticed his car parked at the side of the house. He stopped with a confused look on his face, rubbed his jaw and stared. There were puddles of soapy water on the ground and he could see that someone had given it a good wash. Just then Johnny Bob came around the corner carrying a stack of bath towels. He grinned at Toot and started drying the car.

"How... did the car get back here?" Toot inquired, hoping Johnny Bob hadn't done something rash. "You didn't..."

"Harv Maxwell brought it back about an hour ago... along with the thirty two hundred dollars you won on that last fight."

"But I didn't..." Toot leaned back up against the pickup.

"Harv said you called the odds... not laid them – you were betting **on** Delbert's rooster, not against him."

"But, I..." Toot was feeling a little weak.

"He said you just came over after the fight and throwed two hundred dollars and the car keys in his lap and took off outside. He knew you'd been drinking, said he tried to catch you but you disappeared in the parking lot. He would have brought it back early this morning if he'd a known where you lived. Gambler or not... I think he's a real gentleman."

Toot ran his hand over the car's fender and looked off up the lane, where the sun was going down in a golden haze. "Most of the real gamblers I've known were gentlemen," he said quietly.

"Oh, Norma Jean called and wanted to know if we'd care to go for some catfish and a movie later... I told her I thought we would."

Kings Tonight

The stove glows red
in the herders tent,
somewhere... just west
of the divide.

icy pellets,
driven by a nasty wind
slap canvas
make me think of home

horse blankets and saddles
make fine couches though,
the herder knows no better
poor folks have poor ways

what luck, to find this camp
in early winter blizzard that
no man could foresee.
I shiver at the alternative

"Joaquine" he says, "from Peru"
exhausting his supply of English.
we settle on a bastard Spanish
...his no better than mine

 a leg of lamb hangs by a wire
just above his crackling stove
dripping savory juices
into a boiling can below

just to one side bread
rises in a pan waiting
for the fire to die
enough to use the oven

blackberry brandy
from a saddle bag
is passed back and forth
'til we become old friends

while the wind howls
he tells me of Peru
...Laughing softly
over mugs of steaming coffee

he lifts his head, listens
to ancient murmurings
within the storm... and
knows we have all night

he takes his time now
...the words hanging
like Peruvian Condors
above the Andes

there's much I need to know,
he thinks
about his village
below Machu Pichu

he serves the bread and lamb
on tin plates ...smiling shyly

he apologizes
for the poorness of the fare.

secretly I know
that somewhere tonight,
there are kings
who fare no better

the stove glows red
and I know all
I need to know
about Peru

A Small Good Thing

Doroteo Arango stirs the small pot of beans in a gentle, circular motion. Giving the ladle a little upward twist that will bring the rich bottom layer swirling to the top, this lest they lie too heavily on one another and scorch. Each few minutes he opens the warped, sheet metal door of the oven, and checks the bread.

Snapping off a few twigs from a pile, he feeds them carefully through the vent hole. A good portion of his life has been spent cooking on such a stove and he is aware of its vagaries. He can't remember when he last burned something ...years perhaps. Doroteo enjoys his meals, and simple though they may be, he takes pride in their preparation. Perfection, he knows, comes at the cost of constant vigilance – little enough to pay for something that's exactly right.

A wisp of wood smoke from the damper sends the sweet smell of Aspen through the tent and he notes the wind rising, drawing at the stove pipe, causing it to moan softly. Perhaps it will come tonight, he thinks. He will not let himself be frightened – he knows now that it is just a matter of time. He strokes the little leather pouch about his neck and mutters a quick blessing.

The soft noises of the sheep come from the bed-ground below camp and from the open flap he watches the dog, on the far side of the band, making a slow, wide, gather. "Good'a dog you," he says softly, smiling as the dog does what is in him to do, edging in the stragglers, imperceptibly tightening the band, as they settle for the night. The dog has no name. He was issued to Doroteo along with the camp and the two horses, also nameless. Not unusual, but it bothers him. They will have names, in time, of course, but for now he calls them "dog" or "horse" or "boy", thinking this little bit of English will bind them to him more quickly. He has reached the first of the timberline camps, a small alpine basin, lying at the edge of a sheer drop which falls away into the vastness of the canyon. He is at nine thousand... maybe ten thousand feet, with the snow-fields of Angel Peak rising behind him. The tiny freshet of icy blue glacier-water gurgles past almost reluctantly, as though gathering itself for its final plunge.

All day as Doroteo had pushed the band upward, he watched the feathery ribbon of water cascading off the rim at the head of the canyon, thinking how it would taste at the end of the long dusty climb ...so cold it burns as it goes down, causing your teeth to ache. The coffee and beans you could make with such water ...*Dios mio* ...glacier water ...nothing like it.

This is his first season under the new owner, though he has herded here for some years ...eleven, no, twelve years. Yes, he is certain it has been twelve years. He returns to Mexico only every other year. That is the deal ...every other year. It will be time to go back again this fall, but probably he won't go. Probably he will lay drunk for two weeks down in Anton Chico where there is an old man he once herded with, too old now to follow the sheep. One of the rare ones who saved enough money for a little house, down where the winters are mild, allowing an old man to take his ease. He has invited Doroteo to come visit ...even for the winter should he take a notion. The old man knows Doroteo likely won't stay the winter, but he looks forward to the drunk anyway. It will be good Doroteo thinks, to be with his own kind and speak in his own tongue of the things he knows best ...and then there is the niece from Chihuahua. She comes to take care of the old man, hoping to get her hands on the house someday. She is not young or good-looking, from a town point of view, but Doroteo thinks of her sometimes, there in the mountains, and in his mind's eye she appears in a much more favorable light. She is not, by any stretch of the imagination, as comely as his used-to-be-wife in Chiapas ...that *ingraceada*! ...*puta*! He thinks of all the U.S. Postal money orders he has sent to buy them a little place. Nothing fancy ...a small adobe and a couple of milpas ...maybe a little ditch water for the dry months, something to keep the corn and beans going till the he-rains come in July. But no ...that *bruja*! Carlos Mendoza is now enjoying the fruits of twelve years labor, while Doroteo Arango has nothing to look forward to but a two-week drunk with an old man in Anton Chico ...and perhaps a short dalliance with his ugly niece, who looks out only for herself.

Carlos Mendoza, with whom, he played as a child, whose family was weak and fearful, causing Carlos to be afraid to go North with the others. So now, this ...this ...ner'-do-well, sits in a fine house, with his new woman, stroking his little pencil mustache and looking out over Doroteo's burgeoning fields. This is the picture that comes to Doroteo's mind when he thinks of them together in Chiapas, and he builds upon it in the evenings around the stove – making the house finer and the fields more bountiful each time. He try's never to think of them together in any other setting, in bed for instance, as this would be too much.

He lights the gas lantern hanging from the ridgepole; though the sun has barely gone down, and there is still plenty of light in the white canvas tent. The lantern is only a one-mantle and the difference it makes will be indiscernible for a while yet. A little chill runs down Doroteo's back in spite of the warmth from the stove. There is the muted sound of distant thunder. He listens again to the wind. It has switched, and is now coming out of the South ...unusual for the time of year. He is almost certain it will come now. South, is the direction it would come from.

The round loaf is taken from the oven at exactly the right moment and is set upon a flat rock below the stove to keep warm. Darkness begins seeping through the tent flap, slowly, inexorably, filling every corner, piling up behind every box and bag, making black puddles beneath the stove and table – challenging the little lantern to give a better account of itself.

Doroteo arranges his food on the makeshift table fashioned from pack-boxes. Pouring himself a cup of coffee from the steaming pot he seats himself on his bedroll with a sigh. This is usually the best time of day ...the time he thinks most of when he is in town. He dips his oversize spoon into the enamel bowl of pinto beans, shimmering with tiny ivory globules of fat from the salt pork and bejeweled with the fiery flakes of red chile. Almost smiling, he savors the velvety goodness. You would think a man who has eaten beans nearly every day of his life would tire of them, but somehow he never does. He does, however, look forward to the canned peaches and store-bought cookies he found hiding in one corner of the grub box. This new owner is not so tight of pocket, like the old Greek. That old Greek would never have bought cookies.

Night comes quickly in the mountains and soon the little lantern is spitting and hissing in a valiant effort to keep the darkness at bay – now there is only a small aura of light around Doroteo and the stove – the rest of the tent having succumbed to the somber. Shadows leap and crawl about the walls though Doroteo himself remains motionless. It is the wind on the canvas he thinks ...he hopes. If only he had returned home last year when first he heard the rumors, maybe something could have been done to set things straight. Possibly he could have dealt with Carlos Mendoza in a more reasonable fashion. But he was allowed to go home only every other year. That was the deal. So now it has come to this ...this matter of the Brujas ...the witches.

There is a light tug at the front corner of the tent sending a tremor up the stovepipe, causing the damper to rattle. Doroteo stops eating momentarily, his spoon half-way to his mouth; his night horse testing his lead rope against the Quakie sapling, the same dwarf tree to which Doroteo has tied the corner rope of the tent. Not a good thing to do under ordinary circumstances, but this night horse might be his last warning should the dog be eluded. It is well known that animals can see beyond the realm of man.

The new owner had prevailed upon him to take three horses: one to pack the camp, one for supplies, and one to ride. Doroteo, however, wouldn't hear of it, preferring to walk and lead the two packhorses. In the mountains three horses are twice as much trouble as two. With two horses, one can be turned loose to graze without fear of his leaving the other. Two loose horses, on the other hand, might form a conspiracy and are not to be trusted. In any case, the sheep, many of them young lambs, were slow to climb the mountain and he had no trouble keeping up. Now, in camp in the high country, he will ride once again, should he be of a mind, but always, one horse must be tied. Tonight he has chosen the young buckskin gelding who has the essence of a mustang about him. The other, an older piebald mare, grazes nervously by the stream, unwilling to let the gelding out of her sight.

He finishes his beans, mopping up the last of the rich juice with a wedge of warm bread. An icy draft from the snowfields fingers its way under the flap and Doroteo peers sharply at the black slit. Trembling, he moves closer to the stove, whispering to himself, "...*hacen frio.*" He shudders to think what a close call he might have had, should his cousin Serfin, the one-eyed camp tender, not returned from his leave in Chiapas with word. Serfin – who had come North with him even as boys – riding into camp at dusk last night, his horses lathered and blowing snot from their nostrils.

He had wanted to catch Doroteo before he started the ascent he said, as though apologizing for the state of his animals. He had brought something more urgent than supplies he whispered ominously, rolling his one good eye – the white of it flashing fearfully – as he looked about this way and that, in the shadows of the trees. "It is your wife, Pancloafia, and that... Carlos Mendoza," he said, spitting the name through his teeth. "They have gone to the *Brujas* about you!" He kicked some dirt with the toe of his boot and went on, more softly. "But, you are not alone in this '*Primo,*' my father has sent you something to protect you!" He brought forth a small, black goatskin bag on a leather thong which he placed about Doroteo's neck. "You are not to take it off," he said sharply, "nor look inside!"

Doroteo offered him food and hot coffee, but Serfin just shook his head as he unloaded the supplies. He would not stay the night, choosing instead the comparative safety of the dark, hazardous, trail back down the valley. Preferring the Devil he knew, to one he didn't ...as they say in Mexico.

A grim smile of satisfaction is on Doroteo's lips now, as he grasps the little bag in one hand and shakes his fist to the South. "I am ready...*Bruja*!" he calls into the night, "Ta listos!" Causing the buckskin gelding to pull back on his lead once more, shivering the stovepipe, whose rattle echoes in the tent like a medicine gourd – as if to ward off the evil thing winging its way up the spine of the Sierra Madres.

It must have cost them a pretty penny to have the old witch-woman conjure up such an awesome demon. They are afraid, he thinks, afraid he might come back and cause trouble – try to get something from them – do them some harm. The Arangos are a strong and ancient clan, well known for their swift vengeance, should they feel wronged.

Doroteo knew even before the message came that something bad was afoot; had not a *tecolote*, an owl, sat in the spruce tree above his camp, hooting well into the night ...the worst possible omen. Already, Doroteo can feel, his relations in Chiapas have not been idle. His uncle is a powerful healer himself and has spent many years fighting the spells of the *"brujas malas"*. Certainly he will leave no stone unturned in the cause of his own nephew. Once again Doroteo clutches the black leather bag, feeling inside it the hard, dry thing, which must indeed be a powerful charm.

The wind is on the rise now, causing the stove to draw savagely, woofing into the night like a wild beast as Doroteo loads it with pine knots and aspen knees. The open vent flings dancing red reflections on the canvas walls, warring on the black shadows, driving them back to the farthest corners. Always it is thus, Doroteo thinks vaguely ...light doing battle with darkness ...good opposing evil.

There is thunder close by now, and a brilliant crow's foot of lightning flickers on the tent wall. Huge splashing drops of rain begin pounding the tent with the force of small stones, slowly at first, then building to a crashing cacophony as the violence of the storm funnels down upon the basin. He should be with the sheep, helping the dog. But he is powerless against the force of evil that he knows is at last upon him.

Suddenly the buckskin gelding screams into the wind, viciously shaking the tent, as he rears and strikes at the slight tree. It has come. There is the distant sound of pounding hooves. Instinctively, Doroteo knows the mare is running before the storm. Even the herd instinct will not hold her in the face of such evil. He hears the dog yapping faintly above the wind, beside himself with worry for the sheep. It is as he thought ...the dog ...it has eluded the dog. Oh treacherous demons!

The lantern swings wildly, the tent swaying and pitching as though a ship upon the sea, the ground all but rolling under his feet. Doroteo's mind becomes a vortex, whirling dizzyingly faster in spiraling hopelessness. He feels himself becoming weightless, floating, even as his still ridged body drenched in cold sweat, every vessel throbbing, strains against the all-encompassing evil that sucks at his very soul. Again and again lightning casts its spidery web across the basin, cracking horrendously against the granite walls, illuminating the night in its harsh patina. Inside the tent a tenuous blue aura of fire dances along the ridgepole bringing with it an odor of brimstone, and the whisper of ...death.

Doroteo hears a high wavering voice that he knows must be his own, calling down exorcisms, "...*Espiritos santos*..." Clutching the small leather bag he beseeches, implores, pleads, "...*Por favor ...Dios de cielo*!" he sobs!

The leather pouch seems to pulse as he grasps it ever tighter – the thing within coming to its power now. He feels the surge of virility emanating from this ...this ...talisman. (What can it be to generate such energy in the face of so overpowering a wickedness) Doroteo feels himself coming together, his mind once more in sync with his surroundings, his voice once again connected to his thoughts. He becomes more vehement in his invocations, bringing to bear the name of every saint he can conjure up. Calling upon ever more powerful deities, some of them from the most primitive cortex of his mind, so careless is he now in his growing strength; sensing he will prevail. He fights on, not for the sake of himself, or love, or family, but for victory ...that good should triumph over evil.

Late into the night the tempest rages about him as he kneels there in the mud of the tent floor, praying, until, toward morning, the fierceness of the storm abates. The last vestige of rain died away to a light patter, then stopped altogether. Doroteo emerges from the tent into the breaking dawn where he perceives a world washed clean, where the breeze from the valley floor seems to bring fresh hope. There are the sheep, huddled against the back wall of the basin. The dog paces back and forth in front of the band, holding them, shielding them, from the fate that might have been theirs – had it not been for the power in the small good thing about Doroteo's neck. "Good'a boy you," he calls to the dog. The buck-skin gelding is standing with his head down, trembling, worn out, the tree devoid of bark and limbs from his nightlong struggle. Doroteo caresses his neck and speaks soothingly to him in Spanish. Somewhere in the distance there comes the whinny of the mare, picking her way back up the trail from below.

Doroteo moves among the rivulets of water to the edge of the precipice before the camp. There, looking out over the valley below, and jumble of mountains to the West, he feels the first rays of the new sun through the breaking clouds. He reaches for the little pouch around his neck and with a jerk, pulls it away, tearing the seam at the top. He stares at the bag as daybreak floods the basin with light. Slowly he empties the pouch into his right hand and as a soft breeze brings to his nostrils the warm smell of sun on pine, he examines the shriveled black object he is holding. A cautious smile plays about the corners of his mouth, widening finally to a grin and then Doroteo laughs out loud, the echoes of it resounding from the granite cliffs. Carlos Mendoza will be missing this thing he thinks – and he is not the only one. With a mighty effort he flings it far out into the canyon, its power drained, its magic forever dissipated. Those Arangos, he smiles, take care of their own. He shades his eyes and waves a signal to the dog, who begins moving the sheep toward him. There is good grass here along the rough edges of the rim. As he watches the undulating white blanket flowing across the basin, a great fullness is upon him. In the fall, when his contract is up, he will return to Chiapas. He longs to set with his woman, in his fine home ...looking out across his burgeoning fields.

There Ain't No Trail

The autumn winds were talk'n snow
and blow'n from the North.
I felt the old man tremble
as I put him on his horse.

I 'preciate your time and trouble,
he said, a study'n one old glove.
Think nothin' of it pardner,
them two things I've plenty of.

He raised his head and smiled at me,
I ...I had to look away.
I don't know where the years have gone.
I thought I heard him say.

Well, I knowed I shouldn't brought him,
too old, too weak, too frail...
but he had been a mighty hunter,
and he wanted one last trail.

I cussed the ponies into line...
we started up the track.
The old man, natural, took the lead
and I brought up the back.

He said he knowed a country…
in the Never Summer range.
Where elk growed horns like cedar trees
…back in his younger days.

He sat his pony straight and tall
the way a cowboy rode.
Slippin' sideways in the saddle
To check each horses load

He picked a trail where none had been,
it made a feller wonder…
what kind of man he must have been
…back then when he was younger.

It was canyon walls and waterfalls
and crumbly narrow ledges.
Then up the devil's staircase,
kick'n ice off of the edges.

Rock and slide got in his way,
he paid 'em all no mind.
Just steady kept a climb'n
till we reached the timberline.

He stopped to let the ponies blow
and called me to the rise.
I asked him where the trail had gone?
…and saw him look surprised.

Son, he says, they ain't no trail.
It's just a way of go'n.
Some men never find their way,
yet some seem born a know'n.

There's price to pay, I heard him say
it's sometimes fearsome high!
But them that pays it finds the way
and knows the reason why.

Everything in life's that way
at least I've found it so.
There won't always be a trail
or easy way to go.

The old man's gone these many years
that trip was long ago.
But I still think about him…in the Autumn
when the North winds talk'n snow.

About The Author

Writer, sailor, poet, R. Allen Chappell, grew-up amid the ethnic diversity of New Mexico, where most of these stories are set. He has long been an ardent student of Southwestern archeology and anthropology. A self-admitted outlier, he now lives in Western Colorado where he says, "There is some shade ...and shelter from the interminable wind." He welcomes comments or questions at: rallenchappell@yahoo.com